## IF SHE HAD REALLY FALLEN

down those stairs, how could she have gotten a bump on the back of her head? And what had happened to make her feel that she had seen a man—a man leading a goat down a fashionable London street on which, she was certain, she had never walked?

In her determined search for the solution to a frightening puzzle, Jody Hern finds the true meaning of love.

---

### THE YELLOW BRICK ROAD

# ELIZABETH CADELL
# THE YELLOW BRICK ROAD

BANTAM BOOKS
TORONTO · NEW YORK · LONDON

*This low-priced Bantam Book
has been completely reset in a type face
designed for easy reading, and was printed
from new plates. It contains the complete
text of the original hard-cover edition.*
NOT ONE WORD HAS BEEN OMITTED.

THE YELLOW BRICK ROAD

*A Bantam Book / published by arrangement with
William Morrow & Company, Inc.*

PRINTING HISTORY

*Morrow edition published May 1960*
2nd printing ... September 1960    3rd printing ... November 1961
*4th printing ..... February 1962*
*Condensation appeared in* LADIES' HOME JOURNAL *March 1960*
*Bantam edition published March 1969*

*All rights reserved.
Copyright © 1959, 1960 by Elizabeth Cadell.
No part of this book may be reproduced in any form, by
mimeograph or any other means, without permission.
For information address: William Morrow & Company, Inc.,
425 Park Avenue South, New York, N.Y. 10016.*

*Published simultaneously in the United States and Canada*

*Bantam Books are published by Bantam Books, Inc., a subsidiary
of Grosset & Dunlap, Inc. Its trade-mark, consisting of the words
"Bantam Books" and the portrayal of a bantam, is registered in the
United States Patent Office and in other countries. Marca Registrada.
Bantam Books, Inc., 271 Madison Avenue, New York, N.Y. 10016.*

PRINTED IN THE UNITED STATES OF AMERICA

"Follow the yellow brick road."

THE WIZARD OF OZ

# THE YELLOW BRICK ROAD

# CHAPTER
# 1

THE GIRL SITTING at the dressing table finished combing her hair, put down the comb and then sat for a few moments staring at her reflection.

On the whole, she mused, leaning forward to peer more closely; on the whole, she didn't look too bad. Her color had come back. The dragged look had gone. Also gone, to her relief, was the odd, frightened stare that had confronted her when she had looked at herself two days ago.

She was better. She was back to normal. All was well.

Standing up and looking round the familiar room, she did her best to persuade herself that all was indeed well. What had happened was over; the doctor, who had just paid his last visit, had paused at the door on his way out to tell her emphatically that the sooner she forgot about the incident, the better it would be. The thing to do, he stressed, was to forget; to put the whole unfortunate matter out of her mind; to go back to her job without any of these uneasy, over-the-shoulder glances he had noticed. She must, he insisted, wagging a horny forefinger, rid herself of her absurd suspicions that there had been anything strange, anything sinister connected with the affair. Nothing of the kind. That sort of thing happened every day, and she had been lucky to come out of it with nothing more than a slight head wound. She had fallen down a flight of stairs; she had been found and picked up and restored to consciousness and brought home and put to bed for a couple of days—and now she could get up and take up things where she had left them, and be more careful in future, and good morning to you.

She was better. Her reflection proved it. She was ready to go back to work. And the sooner she got downstairs, the sooner her sister, Estelle, could stop carrying trays up and down. There was enough work in the house without that.

1

She walked out of the room into a long, low corridor and went through a door that led to a gallery. Here she paused, as she paused almost every time she passed this way, to look at the beautiful hall below, with its gray, immensely thick stone walls, its high Gothic windows, its decorated ceiling. It was easy to understand her brother-in-law, Michael Page's pride as he led prospective parents across the smooth lawns separating the school from his house, and ushered them into this lovely old hall. She had heard often enough their admiring exclamations, and Michael's replies, given in his calmest, coolest, most Headmaster-like manner to questions on period and style. Twelfth-century foundations—

—and twelfth-century amenities, reflected Jody Hern, going down the wide, shallow, shining uncarpeted stairs. There were two pictures presented to the world, and both were out of focus. Strangers saw the Headmaster, thirty-five, tall, handsome, urbane, playing host in the historic library and dropping the names of titled pupils casually into the conversation—but Jody knew that while his words expressed concern for the well-being of the boys, his mind ran solely upon fees. His wife, Estelle, looked competent enough in the vast, outdated kitchen, with its spit large enough to roast an ox, a fireplace built to burn whole trees, and a trestle table long enough to accommodate twenty scullions—but Jody knew that Estelle's mind was not on meals, but on music. On these foundations rested Broome Abbey, an establishment of eighty small boys, ten masters and two matrons, with the addition of the Headmaster's own family of twin boys of seven, and a girl of five.

Jody opened the kitchen door. At the far end of the table —she looked half a mile away—Estelle stood absent-mindedly pouring milk onto the contents of a ready-mix cake package. As Jody entered, she looked up and gave an exclamation in which surprise and relief were equally evident.

"Jody! What made you come down? The doctor said you were in bed."

"He told me I was better—and so I am," said Jody. "I don't have to stay in bed indefinitely just because I got a crack on the head. How've you been getting on?"

There was no need to ask. Looking round, she could see for herself the results of her sister's efforts to do the cooking unaided. There were a number of uneaten dishes, three burned saucepans, and evidences of several recipes attempted and abandoned.

Her eyes rested on a gap between two enormous, old-fashioned cupboards.

"Estelle, what's become of the fridge?"

Estelle's face, pale, oval, Madonna-like, lost a little of its habitual calm.

"They . . . they came and took it away," she said.

"You mean you didn't pay the installments?"

"I . . . well, no. It looked so terribly out of place, Jody," she pleaded.

Jody had nothing to say. Four years ago, at the age of twenty, she had answered Michael Page's appeal to leave London and come down to Broome to help to run his house. Servants, easily obtained for the school, with its modernized buildings and its up-to-date equipment, would not work for a day in Estelle's archaic kitchen, and Estelle herself, though eager and energetic, was incapable of organization. She planned meals, knitted for her husband and the children, cut out dresses for her daughter, joined every organization run by the school or the nearby village of Broome, and offered a helping hand to all in need. But the meals were never cooked, the knitting and needlework never finished; committees and the needy waited in vain. Only in one sphere did she achieve proficiency: she was a brilliant pianist, and her drawing room had become the center of the musical society of the district.

Jody now lived at Broome and worked in London as one of a team of girls who visited clients in their homes and gave them the famous and expensive Hortense Beauty Treatment. She combined her two jobs—in London and at Broome—with the calm, unflurried efficiency that characterized her. Between Estelle and herself there was understanding and harmony; Estelle never forgot that it was to Jody that she owed the comfort and smooth running of her home, and Jody never ceased to marvel at a woman who could memorize intricate and interminable sonatas or piano concertos, and forget to order the fish for lunch.

From time to time, Jody installed labor-saving devices; Estelle, appalled by their brash modernity, threw them out again. This was the fourth; the washing machine had gone, and then the spin-dryer and then the electric stove. They were bought on the installment plan, and not the least of Estelle's pleasure in seeing them removed came from the knowledge that they were removed at the company's expense.

"It looked so wrong, Jody," she pleaded. "It looked so terribly out of place."

Jody's eyes rested on her in amusement.

"So do you," she commented.

Estelle leaned against the table and studied her sister thoughtfully.

"When you were in bed," she said, "I made up my mind that it was time I took over. After all, I'm twenty-nine, and it's time I stopped letting you waste your time going backwards and forwards every day, just to keep this household together. I wanted to prove that I could take over."

"Well, you haven't proved it," said Jody. She took an apron from a drawer and tied it round her waist. "Anything I can use for lunch?"

Estelle peered into cupboards and produced some tins.

"You've forgotten to put on your engagement ring again," she said, as she put them on the table.

Jody glanced down at her hand.

"So I have. Funny; you'd think I'd remember, wouldn't you, after four months? Has Charles rung up yet?"

Estelle gave her a brief, uneasy glance.

"He was here this morning," she said.

Jody turned and looked at her in surprise.

"You mean he came? Then why on earth didn't he come up and see me?"

"The doctor was with you, so he waited. And while he was waiting, Michael came in and they . . . they had a talk."

Jody took in the signs of uneasiness.

"You mean they had another quarrel?"

"Yes."

"Same old quarrel?"

"Yes."

Jody frowned.

"Why can't Michael see that other men can be as pigheaded as he is?" she asked wonderingly. "He knows that nobody can push Charles around."

"Yes, he knows . . . but Jody, he needs that money so

badly. It isn't a loan he wants—he's offering Charles a share in the school and—"

"—and Charles doesn't want it. All Charles wants, as Michael knows perfectly well, is to save up enough to give up teaching. He's doing a lot of extra coaching—which he loathes—solely in order to be able to put money aside; he isn't doing it to give Michael a chance to enlarge the school."

"I know that. And I'm perfectly happy to have the school the size it is," said Estelle, "but—"

"—but Michael has just begun to make it pay, and now he wants to have more boys and more buildings and make a fortune in a hurry. Well, I hope he does—but you can tell him that Charles doesn't care a hoot for the school, apart from drawing his salary every term."

"He knows that, but I think he thought he'd have one last try. And Charles got angry and went off in a rage."

Jody grinned. Charles—dark, stocky, strong and not blessed with patience—could very easily go off in a rage. She could picture him: lips compressed, winged brows drawn together and the angry red showing through his tan.

He was the science master at the school. During the term, she saw him on most evenings—but now that the summer holidays were in progress, they met less frequently. He lived on his boat, *Gazelle*, which he kept at Marcove, a tiny harbor about three miles from the school. Science was his living, but sailing was his hobby, his passion, his prime interest. Summer and winter found him aboard, sailing when the weather permitted or in harbor, making *Gazelle* shipshape. He owned a shabby little car in which he drove to Brighton or Eastbourne or London, sometimes staying away for a night or even a weekend in order to give extra lessons. A brilliant teacher, his only desire was to get out of classrooms forever, and live the outdoor life he loved. He was the same age as Michael Page, and the two had been friends all their lives, but lately they had begun to quarrel; Michael wanted a partner, and Charles was the partner he wanted—but Charles wanted only to be free.

Jody did not dwell on the subject.

"I suppose he'll be back when he's cooled down," she said. "Did the boys go off all right?"

"Do you mean the schoolboys or the twins?"

"Both."

"Well, the main school lot went off day before yesterday, and the summer camp ones went yesterday."

"Were the twins excited?"

"Madly."

"And Fenella?"

As usual, mention of her daughter brought a baffled look to Estelle's eyes. Fenella, aged five, with her mother's calm, lovely face and her father's stormy, arrogant disposition, struck fear into more hearts than her mother's.

"Fenella? She . . . she took it awfully badly, Jody."

"I said she would. It's the first time she's been separated from the twins, and it's the first time she's ever come up against something that they can do and she can't. Where is she?"

"Out in the garden. She's been in a furious temper all yesterday and all today. She wouldn't even go up to see you. She started off by kicking all the furniture in her room, but she had on open-toed sandals and—"

Jody laughed.

"I'll go and fetch her in when lunch is ready," she said. "Poor little sweet."

"If you saw her now, you wouldn't call her sweet. Honestly, Jody, I don't know how a child that age can make herself look . . . so forbidding."

"She's lonely, and she can't understand why she couldn't go camping with the boys. I'll talk to her."

She was at the sink, and Estelle walked over and stood by her drying the plates. Then, characteristically, she forgot what she was doing, put down the cloth and began to peer absentmindedly into the saucepans that Jody had set on the stove.

"Who's still at the school?" asked Jody.

"Nobody, thank goodness. Oh well, only the Professor and Miss Bishop. And the Major."

Jody glanced over her shoulder in surprise.

"The Major?"

The music professor, she knew, always stayed during the school holidays. He occupied one of the three little staff cottages close to the house; being a refugee, he had no home to go to, and was allowed to stay at the school. Miss Bishop, his assistant on the staff, had constituted herself his guardian and housekeeper; she lived in the cottage next door to his, and spent the holidays cooking and cleaning for him. But Major Miller was not a member of the staff, and had a cottage of his own, perched on the cliffs above Marcove.

"He's taken on the job of keeping the grounds in order while the gardeners are away," explained Estelle. "The third cottage was empty, and Michael agreed to let him live in it for three weeks."

"Cosy little colony," commented Jody. "The Professor, the Bishop and the Major. You wouldn't have had any hand in arranging it, would you?"

Estelle laughed.

"I did suggest it to Michael," she admitted.

"So now you've got your Trio right on the doorstep. The Professor and his cello, Miss Bishop and her viola, and the Major and his violin. That means music all day and music every evening, I suppose?"

"Yes. Beginning this evening," said Estelle.

"Well, I shan't be here," said Jody.

"Where'll you be?"

"Up in London. I'm going to see Aunt Essie. I'll pack a case and go up and spend the night with her, and go straight to work in the morning."

"You're going back to work?"

"Of course."

"You really feel quite well again?"

"Quite well."

"No more of those peculiar dreams?"

Jody opened her mouth to reply, closed it again, picked up a pile of plates and carried them to the table before answering.

"No more dreams," she said levelly at last.

"I'm so glad." Estelle sounded relieved. "Michael spoke to the doctor, and the doctor told him they were just the result of the knock on the head, and that all you had to do was forget the whole thing. —Oh, Aunt Essie rang up while the doctor was here, and asked about you. She rang up when you were in bed, too, but she said she couldn't get down here to see you."

They both smiled, both being aware that it would take a major disaster to make their aunt overcome her dislike of Michael Page sufficiently to allow her to come to his house.

The sound of a car—no quiet purr, but a familiar sputtering—brought Jody back to the present.

"That's Charles," she said.

She went out of the kitchen and met him in the hall, and felt the peculiar satisfaction that the sight of him always brought her.

He was less tall, less handsome than her brother-in-law, but he had, she knew, a solidity and strength that Michael lacked. He was, for an Englishman, unusually dark, with thick black brows, lashes that a woman might have envied, and a sailor's keen, deep-set eyes. They were vividly blue, and looked striking against his dark, tanned face. His manner was somewhat abrupt, and he was impatient of social graces. His courtship and his proposal had been almost prosaic, but they had suited Jody.

Sometimes she wondered how much she loved him. She felt none of the stirrings of passion, none of the turbulence she had associated with the state of being in love—but Charles satisfied her, and she was happy in his company; that, she felt, was enough.

He saw a girl slender, rather small, not beautiful like Estelle, but with something better than beauty: a look of intelligence, of humor and of sensitiveness. Her nose was small, her mouth rather large; her greatest attraction lay in her dark, laughing, slant-set eyes.

"Better?" he asked.

"Yes." She put up her face for his kiss. "Quite better."

"Good. No more of those hallucinations you were telling me about yesterday?"

Once more the question made Jody hesitate, and then she answered quietly.

"No more," she said, and turned toward the front door. "Come with me; I'm going to look for Fenella."

"What's the matter with Fenella?"

"Her life's blasted. The twins went camping, and she couldn't go. She's taking it hard."

Charles grinned.

"I bet. What's she doing in the garden? Gathering sticks in preparation to burn down the school?"

"I hope not."

They found Fenella hunched on a tree stump near the shrubbery. She replied somewhat coldly to their greetings, and went on to make it clear that she wished to be alone. No, she did not want lunch; as she had not wished to encounter her family, she had had cake and milk with Miss

Bishop, ham sandwiches with the Major and stewed prunes with the Professor. No, she did not wish to come indoors. No, she did not wish to speak to her parents; they had demonstrated only too clearly that they cared only for the welfare of their sons and nothing at all for the happiness of their daughter. She would appreciate it if everybody would leave her alone and allow her to brood upon the world's injustices.

"Well, that's that," said Charles as they walked away. "Time heals all, I daresay."

"You'll stay to lunch?"

He frowned.

"I'm not—"

"You had another row with Michael. So what? Are you going to behave like Fenella?"

"He's a damned persistent—"

"And you're an irritable brute. Chicken salad made with tinned chicken, and cheese soufflé. All right?"

"All right," conceded Charles unwillingly. "Anything you say. Will you come down to the boat afterwards?"

"I can't. I'm going up to see Aunt Essie."

"Why can't you leave her until tomorrow?"

"I'm going back to work tomorrow. I thought I'd take a suitcase and stay the night with her and go straight to work tomorrow morning."

He studied her for a few moments in silence.

"You really feel up to going back to the job?"

"Of course. What's a bump on the head?"

"Nothing . . . unless it leaves you with those peculiar notions you were airing yesterday. Sure they've gone?"

She remembered his face, white and anxious, when he had hurried over to see her when she had returned home after the accident. She had no desire to bring back that look to his eyes.

"They've gone," she said quietly.

She saw his relief, and realized that nothing in her recent accident had caused as much anxiety as her attempts to reconstruct its details. The attempts had been met on all sides with alarm; she had been urged not to look back, not to brood, not to probe uselessly, not to build up a distorted picture.

"Will you drive me to the station after lunch?" she asked.

"Of course."

He took her there, and they sat on the bench on the little platform, hand in hand, saying little. The train came in, and Charles put her into an empty compartment and she was borne away. She leaned back and closed her eyes. Now, at last, she could think. Now, at last . . .

She found, to her dismay, that she did not want to think. As often as she brought her mind to the subject of her accident, it shied away, until at last she gave up the attempt and acknowledged to herself a fact that she had hitherto refused to face: she was afraid to think too much. She was afraid to look too deeply into the fog that obscured the details connected with her accident. She did not know why she was afraid; she only knew that she had come back to consciousness filled with a nameless dread, and though it had lessened, it had not gone away. She was afraid—and she did not know what she was afraid of.

She stared out of the train window and longed to talk to her cool, composed aunt. She could pour out to her all the confused impressions that were filling her mind; Aunt Essie would listen and judge whether any of it was worth investigating.

She reached London and made her way to her aunt's home in Knightsbridge—a house built in Queen Anne style, but so tiny that, standing as it did between two vast newly erected buildings, it looked like a pretty little girl poised between uncouth parents. Her aunt's elderly maid, Clarice, opened the door and led her into the drawing room, and Jody stood looking round the familiar furnishings.

The door opened, and she turned. Her aunt came into the room, and they greeted one another with genuine affection.

Lady Cleeve was about fifty, tall, thin and inexpressibly elegant. Her face, like Estelle's, had a pure, calm beauty, and her manner matched it; Jody had seldom seen her shaken out of her composure. Lady Cleeve had only one expression: a faint look of expectation. "Come on—bore me," she seemed to say—and most people did.

She was a genuine man-hater. At no time in her life had she lacked admirers, but she had only one passion: for orderliness. She loved to surround herself with beautiful things— but the beauty was of a fragile and feminine kind, and in the type of home she had created, men had no place. She thought their persons coarse, their instincts deplorable and their company uninteresting.

Once—unwillingly, tentatively, like a person sipping a drink that others have declared delicious—she married. At the end of four months, her worst suspicions confirmed, she thanked the Earl for his kindness and forbearance, expressed her regret and said that she would really not mind if she never saw him again. There had been no divorce, though Essie had been willing enough to grant one. The Earl now lived abroad and on his infrequent visits to England was sometimes permitted to sit for half an hour in the drawing room at Knightsbridge—and then Essie would rise and offer a cheek and ring for Clarice and have him shown out.

She pitied, deeply and sincerely, her married friends, especially those among them who, since the disappearance of servants, found themselves in the humiliating position of having to minister to their menfolk. They had been lured into marriage by strange biological urges, and there they were, stuck with husbands. Not for them the delicious little salads of asparagus flanked by two halves of tomato; not for them the charm of quiet evenings passed in satisfying solitude, or the cool, uninvaded bed with its silken hangings and a bedroom whose door was opened only to admit the morning tea. The poor things, however, had made their marriage beds and they must lie on them.

For her two nieces—one of them named after her—Lady Cleeve had deep affection, but Estelle exasperated her, and between herself and Michael Page there had long been open war. She had never liked him, but she had ceased to visit them ever since he had persuaded Jody to give up her rooms in London and go down to live at Broome.

She put her hands on Jody's shoulders and studied her.

"Darling, let me look at you. Are you quite better?"

"I'm absolutely all right."

"I worried about you, but Estelle said it was nothing more than a bump on the head. Show me."

Jody bent her head.

"X marks the spot," she said.

"Does it still hurt?" asked Lady Cleeve, peering.

"No. It wasn't very bad."

"I've just sent Clarice out. Come into the kitchen and we'll make some tea and you shall tell me how it happened." She led the way, talking as she went. "You went to give somebody one of the usual beauty treatments, and you fell downstairs and you were found lying in a pool of blood."

Jody filled a kettle.

"Practically no blood," she said. "And I didn't give the treatment because I never got to the client."

"Who was she?"

"I don't know. At least, all I know is her name and the number of the apartment."

"This was at that big block of flats—Dorset Court?"

"Yes. It was the second treatment I had to give that morning; I'd given one from ten to eleven, and then I had to go to an eleven-thirty appointment with Madame Latour at Number Four Dorset Court. But I didn't get there."

"How do you know?"

"Because Madame Latour rang up the office and raised Cain because I hadn't turned up."

"I see. So on the way to Number Four, you fell downstairs?"

"Yes. The elevator was out of order, so I must have walked upstairs. Number Four was only one flight up. I was found by the man who came to mend the elevator."

"How long had you been lying there?"

"It couldn't have been long. The appointment was for eleven-thirty and the last thing I remember was arriving at Dorset Court and checking the time. It was twenty past eleven. I was found at eleven forty-five."

"I see." Lady Cleeve gave her a brief, searching glance. "Those are the facts, and you've come up here to tell me that you're still seeing things quite unconnected with elevators or staircases or clocks?"

"Who told you?"

"Estelle said something about it when I telephoned this morning. She said that you were better, except for a kind of hangover. Is it true?"

"In a way. I came—"

"—because you wanted to say something which you can't say to Estelle, because if you say it to Estelle, she'll pass it on to her husband, who'll pass it on to the doctor, who'll diagnose hallucinations and leave you just where you were. Am I right?"

"Yes."

"Where you're concerned, I'm always right. Take the tray into the drawing room and I'll bring the kettle and then you can begin at the beginning."

She poured the tea, handed a cup to Jody and sat beside her on the sofa.

"Now talk," she directed.

Jody hesitated.

"Perhaps they're right," she said slowly. "But . . ." She leaned forward and spoke earnestly. "No, they're not right, Aunt Essie. I know they're not! The things I see . . . they're not hallucinations. If you dream things, or imagine things, you don't get the clear, vivid pictures I've got in my mind. You don't—"

She stopped as Lady Cleeve raised a long, white, authoritative hand.

"You've begun at the end, not at the beginning," she said. "Suppose you go back to where it all began. Now. You're a young woman employed by a firm of beauty specialists known as Hortense—remember? You go out every day as a qualified member of the staff, giving treatments to rich old women. Three days ago, you looked in your little appointment book and you said: 'This morning I go to Madame le Brun and—'"

"Madame Latour."

"You set out with your little box of preparations—but you never got to Madame's. Is that correct so far?"

Jody frowned.

"I obviously got near her flat," she said, "because the stairs I fell down were the ones just at the end of her corridor. Estelle told me when I got home."

"Michael drove you home?"

"Yes. I was found by the Dorset Court electrician, just at the foot of the stone stairs which lead down from Madame Latour's apartment. The elevator had been reported out of order, and that's why he came along. He fetched people, and I was carried to an empty flat and when I came round, I told them who I was and they rang up home, and Estelle answered and told them where to find Michael—he was at his tailor's in town. So they got hold of him and he drove me home."

"You said the elevator wasn't working. Do you remember that?"

"No. But I suppose I tried it, found it didn't work, and decided to walk up."

"Or you went up in the elevator, which might have been

working when you arrived, and you decided to walk down."

"Why should I walk down before seeing Madame Latour? I obviously got upstairs, or I couldn't have fallen down—but having got upstairs, why didn't I ring Madame Latour's doorbell, tell her I'd come to give her her beauty treatment, and go in and give it? Why?"

"Because—as I pictured it when Estelle rang me up to tell me what had happened—you got there, felt giddy, found the elevator wasn't working, got to the staircase, fainted, fell down the stairs and hit your head on the floor at the bottom."

"I've never fainted in my life."

"There's always a first time."

"All right." Jody spoke calmly. "So I faint. And when I recover, I can remember nothing of my movements from the moment of arriving at the main entrance of Dorset Court. But instead of a blank, which I could understand, my mind's full of . . ."

She stopped. Lady Cleeve, watching her with an anxiety she was careful to conceal, saw her face whiten, and spoke with studied carelessness.

"Now we come to the point," she said. "The hallucinations." Her voice changed, and she spoke gently. "You're worried about them, aren't you?"

Jody stared at her, and her lips trembled.

"I'm . . . I'm frightened, Aunt Essie."

*"Frightened?"*

"Yes. I don't know why. Everybody thinks that having got a knock on the head, it's natural for me to have been left with confused impressions. But these impressions aren't confused. They're absolutely clear. And then suddenly . . . the fear comes."

There was a long silence. Jody sat staring unseeingly across the room; Lady Cleeve sat staring at Jody, remembering the calmness, the humor, the sanity and commonsense that characterized her; recalling her honesty and intelligence and clearsightedness.

"What did you think you saw, Jody?" she asked at last.

Jody looked at her.

"It was a street," she began slowly. "A . . . not a main street, a sort of quiet, small street."

"A London street?"

"Yes. I'm almost sure of that. I saw a row of rather small

houses—small, but not shabby; not mean houses. They looked new, somehow. The whole street looked . . . looked trim, like the better parts of Chelsea."

"All these are only impressions. You said—"

"I'm coming to the clear part. The street is clear enough in my mind, but if I had to put it down on paper, I could only give you a rough idea of it. But . . . there was a man, and the man . . ."

"The man was clear?"

"Absolutely clear. I saw him as plainly as I'm seeing you —only he wasn't as close as you are. He was some distance away, and I watched him coming closer."

"A young man?"

"Yes. A man of about thirty, I think. A man with red hair —the coppery kind."

"Did you watch him for long?"

"No. Because he didn't take more than a few steps, and he was pulling this goat and—"

"*Goat?*"

"You said Estelle told you."

"I didn't think she'd got it right. London street, man with goat . . . it didn't make sense. She also said something about a door."

"Yes. A yellow door. At least"—Jody hesitated, and the color rose in her cheeks—"at least, the top half was yellow and the lower half was black."

Lady Cleeve stared at her for a few moments. Then she replaced her cup on the tray, folded her hands on her lap and spoke thoughtfully.

"I'm keeping an open mind, Jody, but—"

"But you think I'm raving?"

"I said I'm keeping an open mind. But what you're telling me sounds—"

"Crazy. Don't I know? I *know* it all sounds fantastic—but I also know that I saw it. I didn't dream it, I didn't imagine it, and it isn't a sort of vision I had when I was unconscious or half-conscious. I saw it, Aunt Essie. It was real."

"To you." Lady Cleeve picked up Jody's forgotten cup of tea, passed it to her and spoke calmly. "Drink that before it's stone-cold, and listen while I try to make you see this from a few other angles."

"You know that—"

"I know that you're not the hysterical type, if that's what

you were going to say. I know that you wouldn't build up situations out of nothing. But you were unconscious for about forty minutes, I understand, and I think it's only natural that you should have been left with a lot of confused and picturesque impressions. And if overwork had something to do with it—which I'm sure it has—you would be left with a fantasy or two on your mind."

"Fantasy?"

"Fantasy. It's the genuine nightmare recipe, Jody—but I think that if you really try to think about what I've just said, the man and the goat will vanish—and so will the fear you talked about."

"But—"

"But because you believe that you saw something real, telling you that you didn't doesn't help you. And I want to help you—in a practical way. So I'll tell you what we'll do, if you feel it's a good idea: we'll telephone for a taxi and we'll go to Dorset Court and we'll drive right round the block looking for—"

"The yellow door?"

"Yes. If we find the yellow door, I'll swallow the man and the goat. Shall we do that? I mean, would it help?"

Jody's face answered for her; she was on her feet and at the telephone, ringing up for a taxi.

But there was no yellow door. They left the taxi and walked round the four streets that enclosed the great, modern block of apartments. The streets were wide, busy, traffic-filled; the buildings along them were offices or brilliantly lit shops. There were side streets, and they walked down them—but even the side streets were broad and busy. There was no quiet street with a row of small houses.

And there was no yellow-and-black door.

They walked round once, and then again. And then they stood looking at one another, and found nothing to say. The taxi had been sent away, and at her aunt's request, Jody signaled another to take them home.

When they reached the house once more, Jody walked into her bedroom and unpacked her suitcase and Lady Cleeve came to the door and stood watching her.

"I'm sorry about the door," she said at last.

Jody looked up and smiled—the smile that began in her eyes and parted her warm red mouth and made Lady Cleeve feel that nobody was ever lovelier than this young niece of hers.

"I'm sorry too, Aunt Essie. But it was nice of you." She came over and kissed the older woman's cheek. "You tried. You really tried to help—and you tried to believe the story. Nobody else bothered; not even Estelle."

"But you still think you saw the man and the goat and the yellow-and-black door?"

"I don't think," said Jody. "I know. I won't talk about it any more, and I'll go back to work tomorrow and forget the whole thing—I hope. But—"

"But you're sticking to your story?"

"Yes. I saw what I saw," said Jody.

## CHAPTER

## 2

JODY WAS GLAD to be back at her job. The office premises of Hortense were two small airless rooms in an office building in Soho, but she spent very little time there; with the other girls, she received each morning from Hortense—in private life a stout, sensible woman called Mrs. Moore—the letters of clients to be attended that day. She read the letters, copied the names and addresses into her notebook and then went on her round. When time and distance permitted, she walked to her appointments. In summer, she bought sandwiches for lunch and ate them on a bench in one of the parks, or leaning over the embankment watching the traffic on the river.

The work never grew stale. She had tried other jobs, but —like Charles—she had chafed at the day-long confinement. Now she was able to go out, and each client brought a new interest, each address its own surprises. She rang doorbells, thumped knockers and was ushered into little new worlds. There were times when she acknowledged to herself that the job called for very little in the way of initiative, but as jobs went, this one, she felt, was going very well.

Going back after her three days' absence, she determined to put the accident out of her mind, and in some measure succeeded. The picture of the man and the goat remained clear and vivid, but the strange fears associated with them began to fade.

But less than a week later, she had occasion to remember.

She was at Broome, and when she had prepared the dinner, she went into the drawing room to tidy it, for after dinner there was to be music. The String Trio: Professor Joachim, Miss Bishop and her cousin Major Miller: was to play one of the Professor's new compositions. They would come, as usual, about nine o'clock, and Jody would make coffee for them before going up to bed. She seldom stayed to listen; she liked music, but not the Professor's kind of music, which seemed to her to have no recognizable form or tune.

Certainly his works did not provide anybody with a nice tune to whistle. There was nothing for ballad-lovers or jazz fiends. There was, said Lady Cleeve, who had sat through one of the major works at a concert in London, nothing but dreariness and discord. Music critics on the serious newspapers, however, were beginning to accord the works great respect.

The Professor had come to the school from Harrogate, where he had founded the small and struggling Joachim Conservatoire. Arriving unheralded and uninvited, he had asked Michael to give him a place, however humble, on the music staff. The school's head music master had just been fatally injured in a car crash, and although Michael had not yet committed himself, it was generally supposed that he would offer the vacant post to Miss Bishop, for eight years the late master's assistant. But with the sound instinct that seldom failed him in matters relating to the school's prosperity, Michael realized that Professor Joachim, vague, stooping, shabby but the very picture of learning, would make a far greater impression on parents than the humdrum Miss Bishop.

So the Professor was appointed, and a whole page of the prospectus devoted to his attainments. His refugee status was stressed and a veil of esteem thrown over the Joachim Conservatoire, left to struggle on under a deputy. Parents were privileged to hear his latest compositions, played by a newly formed String Trio. A fact that emerged shortly after the Professor's appointment, namely, that he was a very poor teacher, was compensated for by the fact that Miss Bishop was a very good one. The Professor was paraded before the parents, and Miss Bishop got the boys through their examinations.

Her position on the Professor's arrival had been awkward. Almost certain of her appointment as head of the music staff, she had asked the Headmaster if he would consider appointing in a junior capacity a cousin of hers named Major Miller. Michael had agreed to interview him, and Miss Bishop had written to her cousin. She had not seen him for some years, but she had often spoken of him, and so everybody knew him to be about forty, handsome, world-traveled and a first-class violinist.

No written answer came from the Major, but a week after Miss Bishop had posted her proposal, he arrived in person, and by sea, sailing into Marcove in a trim little boat named *Ballerina*. He made his way up to the school, only to learn that there was no post for him.

That was more than a year ago, but the Major was still at Broome, living in a tiny cottage almost at the cliff's edge above Marcove, visiting the school daily and by degrees becoming as familiar a figure as any member of the staff. He played the violin with the Trio, and did a number of useful tasks about the school and its grounds.

Jody liked him, but there were certain things about him which seemed to her inconsistent. Having come in apparent haste to take a junior post, he had stayed on with no post at all. If he had needed money, she argued, how could he have lived for the past year and more without earning any? In his descriptions of his travels, moreover, which he told well, she noted discrepancies of dates and events. What seemed to her strangest of all was the fact that while he showed toward Miss Bishop no trace of rancor for her premature summons, her attitude toward him, in perplexing contrast to the warmth she had displayed before his arrival, was one of unvarying coolness. Jody had once put these points before Charles, and he had laughed at her.

"What are you worrying about?" he had asked. "He's handy about the place, and everybody likes him. If only he'd stop that blasted singing of his, I'd quite like him myself."

"But why should Miss Bishop—"

"She'd like him to push off, I suppose. He reminds her of two hard facts: one, that she didn't get the job and two, that he didn't get the job."

"But wouldn't that make her angry with the Professor, for getting it, or with Michael, for giving it to him?"

"On paper. But in life people usually have it in for anybody they've injured. She brought him here for nothing—so he forgives her, so she doesn't forgive him. Simple."

"But . . . if he can live without working, why did he consider a junior post and—"

"Music, music, music, as the song said. He likes to play his fiddle, and now he's a member of the Trio and gets all the music he wants. What're you trying to do? Find a sinister reason for all this?"

"No. Not sinister. Just sensible. Once, I heard them quarreling."

"Heard who quarreling?"

"Miss Bishop and the Major."

"They're related—let them have rows if they want to," he said lightly. "It's money, I suppose; I wouldn't be surprised if he didn't try to borrow a bit off her now and then."

Between Miss Bishop and the Professor, all was friendly. His childlike blue eyes peered shortsightedly round to find her whenever she left him for long. She copied manuscripts for him, saw that he was on time for his lessons, made sure that he did not—as he had done in his early days at the school—give the lesson by mistake to the wrong pupil. She did his shopping, saw to his linen and generally mothered him. They made an odd pair: he was tall and thin and stooping, and her figure was like an old drawing of a trapeze artist—small waist, billowing hips and bosom, and hair arranged in a loose, old-fashioned style over her brow. Like the Professor she was about fifty; like him, she looked a good deal more.

Tonight the drawing room had an intimate air. There were no guests: no small boys marched over from the school to improve their musical taste, no members of the staff here from a sense of duty. Estelle sat listening, silent and absorbed, and the Trio played.

Jody waited for an interval and then carried in the coffee. She found Michael just entering the drawing room, and he took the tray from her.

"Coming in?" he asked.

"No. Going to bed."

She knew that he envied her, and knew that he would not say so. Much of his success in building up the school had been the care with which he had played his role of Headmaster. Without the smallest knowledge of or interest in music, he had since the Professor's appointment taken pains to learn the patter, and Jody admired the ease with which he relayed it. He had discovered that Ambrosian Modes had nothing to do with fashion; that the Horn family were not human; that Ferrari was not only a racing car, but a composer, conductor and critic. He could refer airily to Joseffy, Stokowski, Inghelbrecht and Franchomme, and he could pronounce Maschinenpauden. Jody had once even heard him telling a group of hypnotized parents that the Professor rarely held to the melodic line.

The Professor came across to speak to Jody, his mild blue eyes beaming with pleasure.

"What is this they tell me?" he asked, in his stumbling English. "You haf fallen somewhere?"

"It was nothing. I fell down some stairs."

"Ah!" The sound was soft, distressed, sympathetic. "I do not hear before; I was away at my Conservatoire, playing to them my last composition. You are quite, quite well now?"

"Quite, thank you. Wasn't that a new composition you were playing just now?"

"New, yes. I finish it only last week. Miss Bishop, the good Miss Bishop has been so kind to copy out the music. Now I am working at something new again."

"But these are the holidays," Jody reminded him.

"For the boys, holidays; for me, no. I am finishing a *muneira*."

"A—?"

"How you would call it? A *gallegade*—you know?"

Miss Bishop came to the rescue.

"Spanish dance," she explained, in her pleasant but abrupt way. She stood beside them in characteristic pose: feet apart, arms folded across her large bosom. "Spanish dance, popular in Galicia. Compound duple time, ta, ta, ra-ta, ra-ta, ta, ta. Interesting. The Professor thinks the boys will enjoy it next term."

Jody felt that the boys would have been much happier with a percussion band, but did not say so.

"You're looking much better," went on Miss Bishop, who had been studying her frankly. "Lost that peaked look. Trouble with falls is that you can't say how long the effects are going to last. A shock's a shock, even when you're young. Be careful if I were you. What happened, exactly?"

"It sounds rather silly," said Jody. "I was found at the bottom of a flight of stairs."

"Absurd part of it," observed Miss Bishop, "is that I was up in London that morning, seeing the school printers. If only your sister had remembered when they rang her up, I could have hopped into a taxi and been with you in two shakes. Pity."

"The Headmaster was in town," explained Jody. "He brought me home."

The Major came to join them; Miss Bishop moved coldly away, and he launched into an account of the plays he had seen on his recent visit to town.

"Dull on the whole," he said. "If the acting was good, the play was bad, and if the play was good, all the original cast had left and the thing was petering out. How's the bump on the cranium?"

"Better, thank you."

"Found by the electrician, I hear, Tck, tck, tck. Never," he admonished, "swoon before you're absolutely certain that a suitable preserver's standing by."

"Please?" begged the Professor.

"I'm telling Miss Hern never to jump off the pier before she's hailed the handsome coastguard."

"She will jump off a pier?"

"No, I won't," interposed Jody. "Professor, some more coffee?"

"No, thank you. No, no," said the Professor. "Thank you, but it is time that we play again, I think."

He carried his cup to the tray, a signal that the interval was over. Jody gathered the empty cups and the Major carried the tray to the kitchen. As she walked across the hall, Jody looked up and caught a glimpse of white at the top of the stairs.

"That's Fenella," she told the Major. "I'll go up and see her."

She went up to her niece's room. Fenella, wide awake, seated cross-legged on her bed, greeted her reproachfully.

"You didn't come," she said. "You said you would."

"I've only just cleared away the coffee cups. What were you doing on the staircase?"

"Looking."

"Well, how about sleeping?" Jody removed some books and toys from the bed and tucked up the small figure.

"Didn't say my prayers," said Fenella, when the operation was completed.

Jody hesitated. Since the departure of her brothers to the summer camp, their names, and the names of her parents, had been dropped from Fenella's devotions, and she had put in instead some requests which must have pained the Recording Angel.

"There's no use in saying prayers," she said cautiously, "unless they're going to be proper ones." She sat on the bed and took a small hand in her own. "Why can't you be a nice girl and pray that the twins will have a lovely time?"

"Cos' they left me behind."

"But Fenella darling, it was a boys' camp, and you're a girl."

"This is a boys' school, and they let me be here," pointed out Fenella.

"Yes, but that's because you're in your own house. In a camp, all the boys have to sleep in tents, and that's all right for little boys but it isn't so good for little girls."

"Why not for?" demanded Fenella.

"Because little boys have to grow up hard and—and tough. But girls—"

Anything boys could do, Fenella broke in to explain, she could do better.

"But that's not the point. Men are men, and girls are girls. Men have to be strong and girls have to be—"

"Mummy says I've got to grow up nice and strong."

"But that's strong in another way."

"What way?"

"Well . . . I'm not very good at explaining."

That, agreed Fenella, jumped to the eye. She ate her cereal every morning solely in order to become strong. Why, then, exclude her from the camp?

"One day you can go to a girls' camp."

At this, Fenella broke down completely.

"I d-don't want to go to a hollible old girls' camp," she howled bitterly. "You can *keep* it!"

Jody gathered her up and hugged her.

"It's hard, my sweetie-pie, but they would have taken you if they could."

"No, they w-wouldn't. They said they d-didn't want any little girls!"

"They were just teasing. And if you'd gone with them, you couldn't have helped me to buy presents for the twins' birthday, could you?"

"They won't be h-here for their birthday."

"No, and so we can have lots of fun packing the parcels. We'll buy them and wrap them up and we'll go into the big post office at Eastbourne and we'll post them off to the—" she almost said camp, and pulled herself up hastily. "Now kneel up and say your prayers."

Fenella knelt on the pillows, clasped her hands and closed

her eyes tightly. Five seconds later, she was snuggling between the sheets.

"That didn't take you long," remarked Jody.

"I said 'Gentle Jesus, Amen.' "

Jody decided that the hour was too late for missionary work. She kissed the flushed little face, left the door open by request so that the light from the corridor would shine into the bedroom, and went downstairs in time to answer the telephone's shrill summons. She picked up the receiver and heard her aunt's voice.

"Is that you, Jody?"

Something unfamiliar, something a little odd in the tone made Jody's hand tighten round the receiver.

"Yes, Aunt Essie."

"Listen to me carefully," said Lady Cleeve. "You remember that extraordinary story you told me the other day?"

"Story?"

"Oh Jody, you know!" Her aunt's cool voice became cooler. "The goat, the man, the door."

Jody stared unseeingly across the hall.

"What is it, Aunt Essie?" she asked.

"It may be nothing; absolutely nothing." Lady Cleeve sounded slightly bewildered. "I may be making an absolute fool of myself—and of you. But I had to ring you up and tell you."

"Tell me what?"

"Tell you that . . ." There was a pause, and then Lady Cleeve spoke again with deliberate calmness. "I'll try to make it absolutely factual, and then you can take it or leave it. Are you listening?"

"Yes."

"Well, I've just got back from London Airport. I went to see a friend off to America, but that doesn't concern you. The part that does concern you is this: I came back on one of the airport coaches and I sat next to a woman whose two friends were sitting on the seat behind us. She spent the entire time talking to them, and you can't help overhearing somebody's conversation if most of it is being screamed into your ear. So I heard, and it was terribly boring and I wished I could change my seat, but I couldn't because the coach was full. And then suddenly I didn't want to move any more. She said something that . . . that galvanized me."

Jody waited.

"She was talking about another woman called Nancy," went on Lady Cleeve. "And suddenly one of her friends from the seat behind said: 'Oh, by the way, how's the goat getting on?' "

"The . . . the goat?" echoed Jody.

"Yes. Don't interrupt, just listen. The woman next to me said . . ." Lady Cleeve's voice broke off, and there was a pause. Jody, frantic, beat a tattoo on the bar of the telephone.

"Hello—hello! Hello!"

"It's all right," came calmly from her aunt. "I haven't gone. I'm just thinking. Jody—can you come up?"

"I can come tomorrow after work. Go on telling me, Aunt Essie."

"I meant can't you come up now?"

"Now? At this time of night?"

"I've just looked at the time; it's ten past ten and you could—if you got Estelle to drive you to the station—catch a train."

"But—"

"Don't argue, Jody; just do as I say."

"But tell me—"

"There's no time to tell you any more. Come up tonight. That is, if you want to. Goodbye."

There was a click. Jody stood staring at the receiver, and then she put it slowly down upon the stand. For some moments she stood motionless—and then she picked up the timetable and flicked through its pages—and then opened the door of the drawing room and beckoned cautiously but urgently to Estelle. Estelle came to the door, and Jody drew her out of the room.

"Will you drive me to the station?" she asked. "Nothing's happened, and everything's all right, but Aunt Essie rang up and—I'll tell you on the way to the station. *Hurry*, Estelle."

Before Estelle had got the car out of the garage, Jody was waiting, her night things bundled into a case. She climbed in beside Estelle, and began a hurried explanation.

"Aunt Essie rang up and said she had something to tell me—"

"About what? Oh!"

Jody turned to stare at her.

"What's the matter?"

"Nothing. I just know what she wants to tell you, that's all. Uncle Bruce is back!"

"That wasn't what she—"

She paused. The Earl of Cleeve, and his periodical visits to England had come to be recognized by Estelle and herself as a time of great trial for their aunt. Estelle thought that this was the reason for this late summons—and it would be as well not to embark upon explanations. The station was in sight and the train could be heard making its way over the hill. Estelle was off on a train of her own—a not unusual proceeding—and to check her and bring her back would take too much time. Jody said no more.

When she reached the flat, it was Lady Cleeve who let her in. She was in a cloud of pale pink nylon; a faint, delicate scent hung in the air. She drew Jody in and closed the door.

"I'm glad you came. Clarice has gone to bed, but if you want any coffee or—"

"No; nothing, thank you."

They sat facing one another on the sofa.

"How far did I get on the telephone?" asked Lady Cleeve. "Coach and conversation—wasn't that it? And then suddenly, this remark about a goat. One woman said to the other: 'Oh, by the way, how's the goat getting on?' I'm not normally interested in goats, but it was what followed that rivited my attention. The other woman said: 'What goat?' and the other woman—did I tell you there were three?—said: 'Don't tell me that Nancy's got a goat! And the first woman said: 'Yes' and the other woman said: 'You're joking.' By this time, of course, I was listening quite openly. It appears that Nancy had got a goat, had had a goat for—note this, Jody—for about a week, and was getting along very well with the goat. Well, it could still have been nothing. They seemed to get tired of talking about the goat. But just as I'd begun to get a deflated feeling, one of the women behind me said—rather thoughtfully: 'I didn't know anyone could keep a goat successfully right in the middle of London.' And I gathered from what they said next that Nancy—whoever Nancy is—has a large garden that stretches much farther than you'd think just by looking at her house. It goes down as far as Waverley Square."

She paused. Jody gazed at her blankly.

"Waverley Square?" she echoed.

"You don't know where it is? Neither did I. So I looked it up." Lady Cleeve rose, floated across the room and returned with a book map of London. "Look. Page forty-two, Square E.4."

Jody was searching in the square indicated.

"Yes, I've got it," she said after a time.

"See where it is?"

"I . . . yes, I see." Jody spoke with bewilderment in her voice. "I see. But what could that possibly have to do with—"

"It's two streets away from Dorset Court. It can't just be coincidence, Jody. About a week ago you saw a goat. I didn't think you had, but now I've changed my mind."

"But I couldn't have—"

"—seen a goat in Waverley Square, if you weren't in Waverley Square?" Lady Cleeve folded her hands calmly in her lap.

"Jody, you could have been there."

"But I remember going to Dorset Court. I got there just after twenty past eleven. I can remember checking the time."

"And after that?"

"After that there's a blank," admitted Jody.

"Then why not assume that you had a sort of blackout and wandered for five or ten minutes? You cross the road at the entrance to Dorset Court"—she leaned over and pointed —"and you walk up that main street and then you turn into Waverley Place. We walked down Waverley Place the other day, but we didn't think of turning into Waverley Square. If we had, I'm quite certain we would have seen your yellow-and-black door."

There was silence for a time, and then Jody shook her head.

"No, Aunt Essie."

"How do you know? And why don't you put it to the test? Get your treatments done in a hurry tomorrow morning, have an early lunch with me, and after lunch we'll both go to Waverley Square and see if there's a yellow door. If there is, there's your explanation."

"Do you think it would make me feel any better to know I'd been wandering round the streets in a daze?"

"It would make me feel better. I don't mind your having blackouts. I've heard of people having them and I can allow you a blackout or two—but I don't ever again want to see on your face the . . . the stricken expression that was on it when you told me about the man and the goat. You looked . . . you looked sick, Jody, and I couldn't bear it. A blackout isn't pleasant, but it's something you can deal with. Nameless fears are something else again—something far more unpleasant. Come with me tomorrow and we'll find your yellow door, and then all those fears of yours will vanish."

"I . . ." Jody stood up. "All right," she said.

"Good."

"And . . . thank you for ringing up."

"Did you tell Estelle?"

"No. She got the idea that Uncle Bruce was in England again, and there wasn't time to explain."

"You can explain when you go back. Tomorrow, twelve-thirty at Frangopoulo's."

But Jody, after all, lunched alone. Lady Cleeve telephoned during the morning: they had spoken of the devil, and the devil had appeared; she was to lunch with her husband and would have to give up the expedition to Waverley Square. Would Jody wait, or go alone?

Jody went alone. Getting off the bus opposite the largest of the four entrances to Dorset Court, she stood for a moment looking at the great block of flats, fighting an inexplicable panic that welled up and threatened to engulf her. She had got out of the bus on that morning not so long ago, and she had walked up to the entrance . . . and then?

She put speculation aside, crossed the road and walked down Waverley Place. The distance was not great; she saw that barely five minutes had elapsed before she had reached the corner and turned into Waverley Square.

She halted, her glance taking in the quiet, wide street—and she saw at once that it was not the street she had seen, or imagined she had seen. These were not the houses she had described to her aunt. Neither in imagination nor in reality had she ever seen Waverley Square.

Her feelings, she found, on examining them, were divided equally between disappointment and relief. She would have liked to be sure . . . but perhaps there were things better left undiscovered. Here, certainly, there was nothing to fear. On both sides stood tall houses; near the place on which she was standing, green branches overhung a high wall behind which children's voices sounded, bringing a comfortable suggestion of safe, enclosed gardens. This was a sober Square, even a noble Square; nobody would have presumed to paint any of these dignified doorways that frivolous shade of yellow.

She turned to go back to the bus stop. She took three steps—and then froze in her tracks.

From the other side of the wall, loud and prolonged and insistent, came the bleat of a goat.

## CHAPTER

# 3

A FULL MINUTE PASSED before Jody moved again—and during that time, silence fell upon the garden on the other side of the wall. The voices of children no longer sounded; the goat, having uttered its complaint, spoke no more.

Her next movements were automatic. She walked forward and came to a low, wooden door in the wall. She pushed it open, entered the garden and stood staring at a small, white tethered goat.

The door closed with a clatter behind her, but she did not hear it. She was taking in the scene before her, observing it intently, absorbed, oblivious to the fact that she was trespassing.

She was in a long, narrow garden that ran parallel to the street along which she had walked from Dorset Court only a few minutes ago. Now she was facing in the opposite direction, and immediately before her was the row of houses—low, single-storied—to which the gardens belonged; beyond, rising above them, towering, she saw the massive structure of Dorset Court—not the block that faced the main entrance, but one which ran at right angles to it. Standing and staring at the endless row of windows, she realized that from one of them—if she had looked out of one of them—she could have seen this goat. This could have been the house to which the goat was being led; she was looking at the side of it that faced the garden, but if she walked round to the front, perhaps there would be a yellow-and-black door. Perhaps . . .

Something moved. Jody turned and, with sickening abruptness, came back to the present. She was trespassing in a stranger's garden. Worse, she had blundered into what she now saw to be a kindergarten: ten or more small children seated in a semicircle round a tall, thin, elderly woman who had risen from her chair and was now bearing down on Jody with outrage written plainly upon her face.

31

Jody eyed her uneasily. Beyond her, she could see the pupils' heads turned in her direction; the chatter that had ceased when the class was resumed now broke out again. An aged gardener paused in his weeding and fixed a watery but suspicious glance on her. A baby, lying against embroidered pillows in something too regal to be termed a pram, rested wide blue eyes on the intruder.

The tall woman halted before Jody, and took a deep breath. It was the prelude, Jody knew, to hostilities. The first salvo came in deep-freeze form.

"May I know what you are doing here?"

For the first time since entering the garden, Jody saw her action from an outsider's point of view. She had burst into a private garden in which the baby had been put to rest, in which young children were settling down to their lessons. She had stood without apology, looking coolly about her. It was no wonder she was being asked—coldly—to present her credentials.

She opened her mouth to give an explanation, but she found, to her dismay, that nothing but lame phrases formed themselves in her mind. She had heard the goat, and she had wondered . . . she had felt . . . there was a rather urgent reason . . .

She struggled to pull herself together. The small, keen eyes resting on her were dark with suspicion.

"I'm sorry. Please forgive me," she said more firmly. "It was a . . . it was a mistake. I only wanted to find out—"

"You are not a friend of Lady Wigram's?" cut in the elderly woman abruptly.

"Lady Wigram? No, I'm afraid not."

"You did not know whose garden this was?"

"No. But, you see, I heard the goat and—"

"Am I to understand that you walked in here simply in order to look at a goat?"

"Well . . . yes." Jody knew that her color was rising and her manner becoming flustered. "It's a rather long story, I'm afraid, but—"

"Then perhaps you will kindly tell it to Lady Wigram," suggested the woman coldly. "She is coming now."

Jody turned. A woman of about thirty—small, pretty, plump and with an expression of calm good humor had come out of the house. Two little boys detached themselves from the other children and ran to meet her, and she paused to pet them and to shoo them back to their places. Then she had come up to Jody and was looking at her with a faint smile.

"The gardener told me I was wanted," she said.

For an old man, he moved fast, thought Jody. Up to the house with news of an intruder, and back to his post to listen in. Spry for his age.

She faced Lady Wigram and spoke with as much composure as she could muster.

"I'm sorry to have burst in so rudely," she said quietly. "I was out there in Waverley Square, and I heard the goat—and before I could stop myself, I'd found the garden door and I was in the garden. I didn't mean to trespass, but . . . but I had a rather special reason for wanting to see the goat."

Lady Wigram, relaxed and friendly, screwed up her eyes in a puzzled way, and laughed.

"It sounds intriguing." She turned to the elderly woman. "It's all right, Miss Bond. Please go on with the class."

"I felt it my duty to make inquiries," said Miss Bond, directing a stern look at Jody. "One hears terrible stories, don't you know. Babies are left in perambulators, and one has to be on the watch."

She gave a stiff bow and went back to her pupils, and Lady Wigram looked at Jody.

"Won't you come into the house?" she asked. "I have to go out in about twenty minutes, but perhaps you could explain about the goat."

"I won't stay, thank you," said Jody. "I trespassed, and it's more than kind of you to forgive me—but I have a job and I ought to be getting back to it. Only . . . something odd happened to me a little while ago, and . . ." She stopped and put a question. "Would you tell me how long you have had the goat?"

"Betsy?" Lady Wigram gave the animal a vague glance. "Oh . . . I'd say just over a week. I can't give you the exact date of her arrival, because I was away." She paused and looked at Jody with a touch of anxiety. "You're rather pale," she said. "Do come into the house and sit down for a little while—then you can tell me quietly and comfortably what made you come in to see Betsy."

Her voice was warm, her manner kind. Jody smiled in gratitude.

"I'm sorry—I really have to get back to work," she said. "But if you would allow me to come this evening—that is, if you're free—"

"I'm free from six to seven. Could you come then?"

"Yes. Thank you," said Jody. "There'll be time to tell you the whole story—but it won't sound very sensible."

They had turned and were walking toward the gate.

"Did you know Betsy before we got her?"

"No. But . . . I saw a goat when . . . You see, my aunt rang up last night, and—"

"She's not the previous owner of Betsy?"

"No. Oh, no. She lives in Knightsbridge—the smallest house in the district, and I don't think a goat could fit. . . ." She stopped. "It's a rather involved story," she ended. "I hope I'll be able to tell it sensibly this evening."

"But"—Lady Wigram had opened the garden door, but was obviously interested and reluctant to let Jody go—"you *have* seen Betsy before?"

"I don't know. That's what I hope to find out tonight. I think I saw her about a week ago when I went to give a beauty treatment to somebody living in Dorset Court."

"Over there?"

Lady Wigram waved a hand.

"Yes. I . . . I think I had a sort of blackout, and . . . when I woke up, I remembered the goat."

"You saw Betsy, you think?"

"Yes. I was on my way to Madame Latour's flat in Dorset Court, and I feel sure that I must have seen the goat from a window nearby and—"

Her voice faltered and died away. On Lady Wigram's face there had appeared suddenly an odd expression. Friendliness, warmth, interest had vanished. How, or why, Jody could not tell—but she was only too well aware that what she was saying was no longer being said to a sympathetic audience. Lady Wigram was still standing with one hand on the garden door. She had said nothing whatsoever, but Jody knew that something she herself had said or done had abruptly changed the other woman's attitude toward her. The look on her face was only too plain: she thought Jody a liar.

There was a short, dreadful silence, during which Jody burned with bewilderment and humiliation. Then Lady Wigram had opened the door wide.

"Goodbye, Miss—"

"Hern. I—"

"Goodbye, Miss Hern." Lady Wigram smiled once more, but it was the cold, scornful smile of a woman reproaching herself for having allowed herself to be taken in. "I'm so sorry I shan't be at home this evening; I've just remembered an engagement."

"I think . . ." faltered Jody.

"Goodbye."

The word, distant, disdainful, was followed by the sound of the door closing. Jody was outside, in Waverley Square, and as she stood, engulfed in shame, she heard the bolts of the door being drawn. No more intruders would gain access.

She walked in a daze to the end of the Square and turned into the main street. Jody reached the bus stop and stood with her head whirling. She had been on the verge of knowledge—and it had been snatched away. She went, word by word, over her short exchange with Lady Wigram, but could discover nothing that could account for the inexplicable change in atmosphere.

On an impulse, she crossed over to a telephone booth and rang up Estelle: she would, she said, stay with her aunt tonight and go home tomorrow, Saturday morning.

"Is Uncle Bruce in town?" Estelle asked.

"Uncle Bruce?" Jody, with an effort, brought her mind from goats and gardens. "Yes, he's here."

"I told you so. It always upsets her. Has she seen him?"

"She lunched with him today."

"You sound odd; you're not overdoing it, are you?"

"No. I'll see you tomorrow," said Jody, and rang off.

She made one more call: to her aunt; then she forced her mind back to her afternoon's appointments.

When she got to the house in Knightsbridge that evening, Lady Cleeve was out. Clarice, leading Jody to the drawing room, said that she would be in soon, and offered to make tea. Jody refused, and sat alone in the quiet, restful room and found the events of the past week rushing back at her with almost overwhelming force.

There was nothing, absolutely nothing, she told herself, to be frightened of—but she knew that she was trembling. Looking down at her hands, she found that they were tightly clasped, one clutching the other so firmly that the knuckles showed white. She could hear the thud of her heart, and knew that fear was returning—the fear which had been with her, in varying degrees, since she had returned to consciousness after her accident.

She was afraid. The terror which had been gradually lulled, which had receded a little, was back again—and now she knew without any doubt that the fear had its roots in the things she had remembered, and which others said that she had imagined: the man, the goat, the yellow-and-black door. She had seen only the goat, and she had hoped to solve the riddle of why and when she had seen it—but now she saw that it would be wiser, safer to put memories behind her forever. She would have to forget. Man, goat, door. From this moment, she swore to herself, she would leave them where they were: in the dark places of her mind. She would leave them, and the nameless fears that attended them, behind her. There must be no more looking back.

The decision taken, she felt better. She got up and went to her bedroom, and as she reached it, she heard sounds on the steps that led up to the front door. Turning back, she called her aunt's name and went to open the door to save her the trouble of using her key.

She opened the door wide, and had uttered the first word of greeting, when she saw that it was not her aunt who stood on the steps.

It was a man—and she had seen him before. He had not been so close, or so clear—but she was in no doubt of who he was. He was the man who had been leading the goat. He had been the man walking toward the yellow-and-black door.

For a few blank seconds, she could only stare—and she felt panic gripping her. She fought it down, and it rose again. Horror seized and held her. She put out a hand to grope for the door, and tried feebly to move it, to shield herself—and then she saw the man take a step forward. Her hand moved, encountered his chest and she made a desperate effort to thrust him from her.

And then she was falling, falling—and she knew, as blackness closed round her, that she was falling into his arms.

# CHAPTER
## 4

SHE OPENED HER EYES to find herself lying on the drawing-room sofa. Two people were bending over her: one was Lady Cleeve, and the other was the man who had been standing on the steps. In the background hovered Clarice, wide-eyed with worry.

For some moments, nobody spoke, and then Lady Cleeve's voice came anxiously.

"How do you feel, Jody?"

Jody sat up slowly.

"I'm . . . all right, thank you," she said. "I'm sorry I was so . . . so stupid."

She looked up at the man. She had remembered him as angry-looking, and he was frowning now, watching her with brown, intent eyes. Once more Lady Cleeve spoke, this time in bewilderment.

"Do you two know one another?"

It was the man who answered.

"I don't think so." He straightened, and his bulk seemed to fill the room. He was over six feet tall, and broad-shouldered, and his hands and feet looked enormous. "I was just about to ring the bell when the door opened and—"

"I thought it was you," Jody told her aunt. "But it wasn't."

"Why should that make you faint?" Lady Cleeve paused and then spoke slowly. "Jody, you don't mean that he's . . . that he's the man you—"

"Yes," said Jody.

The stranger looked from one to the other. Lady Cleeve waved Clarice away and as the door closed behind her, addressed Jody once more.

"You didn't know he was coming?"

"No."

"And when you saw him, you were frightened?"

"Yes."

37

"And you fainted?"

"Yes."

There was a pause.

"I've never been thought handsome," came slowly from the man at last, "but I've never realized that my appearance could frighten a girl into fainting."

"The circumstances," Lady Cleeve told him, "are rather peculiar."

"What did I do to frighten you?" he asked Jody.

"Nothing."

"Then—?"

"It's all rather involved," broke in Lady Cleeve, "and we'd better begin at the beginning." She sat down, and after looking round as though trying to select a chair capable of bearing the weight of the visitor, waved him to one and spoke in her usual calm way.

"Since you were coming to visit me," she began, "I presume that you know who I am." As his embarrassed air proved that he did not, she told him, and he bowed.

"I'm sorry to have come without warning in this way," he said. "I came looking for Miss Hern."

"This is my niece, Joanna Hern."

He looked at Jody.

"You told my sister this afternoon that your aunt lived in a very small house in Knightsbridge—a house too small to hold a goat. I took a chance and came to this one, and I was going to ask if a young lady named Miss Hern lived here."

"I went to Waverley Square after lunch," Jody explained to her aunt.

"I see. And you found the yellow door?"

"No I didn't. And I was just going to walk back to the bus when I heard . . . I heard a goat bleat. It was in a garden just near where I was standing, and before I knew what I was doing, I'd walked in."

"And you talked to my sister, and here I am."

"Any may I ask who you are?" inquired Lady Cleeve.

"I'm sorry. I should have told you. Huntley. Desmond Huntley. Thirty-two, Lieutenant-Commander, Royal Navy, on a month's leave after service in the East, and staying with my sister in Waverley Mews." He hesitated. "If it isn't asking too much, perhaps you'd tell me why I'm mixed up with a goat and a yellow door in a way that frightened your niece?"

"I think it would be better," said Lady Cleeve, "to begin at the beginning."

In a few sentences, she told him of Jody's accident and subsequent conviction that she had seen a man and a goat. She told him of the conversation overheard in the airline coach—and then Desmond Huntley took up the tale.

"Nancy is my sister, Lady Wigram," he explained. "She's got two little boys, and a baby of six months. The baby was ordered goat milk and when I came home on leave about ten days ago, I found her very depressed at having to leave London and go to live in the country, where the goats are. I told her I'd see whether I could induce a goat to come and live in town, and I found one—name of Betsy." He looked at Jody. "And you must have seen me the day I installed it."

"You were pulling the goat along—but there was a door. . . ."

"The yellow door? That's my sister's front door."

"But it was black and yellow."

There was a momentary look of bewilderment on his face, and then he had put his head back and was laughing—a laugh which brought a smile to Jody's lips and sent Lady Cleeve's anxious glance to her ornaments.

"You're quite right—it was black and yellow," he said at last, sobering. "My sister was painting it. She does a lot of amateur decorating, but she can only do the upper half of the doors while the children are around. When they've gone to bed, she does the lower half."

"But we looked for a yellow door in all the streets round Dorset Court," objected Lady Cleeve, "and there wasn't one."

"There wouldn't be," he told her. "My sister lives in Waverley Mews, which is a very narrow cobbled lane between Dorset Street and Waverley Square. Unless you turned off Dorset Street and turned again, you wouldn't see it." He looked at Jody. "Where were you when you saw me with the goat?"

"I don't know." She paused for a moment and then looked directly at him. "Will you tell me what I said or did this afternoon to offend your sister?"

"Offend?" repeated Lady Cleeve in surprise.

"I was talking to her and she was being perfectly friendly," said Jody, "and then quite suddenly, she . . . she froze. It was terrible." She turned to Desmond Huntley. "What did I do?"

He hesitated, and seemed to be choosing his words carefully.

"You didn't do anything," he said. "But something you said made her feel, just for a moment, that you weren't as—as frank as you appeared to be."

"But what did I say?"

"You told her that you saw the goat from a window near Madame Latour's flat."

"Why should that upset her?"

"Because she knows Madame Latour, and visits her frequently. And she knows that her flat is on the other side of the building, quite away from any windows overlooking Waverley Mews. Madame Latour lives on the north side, so that if you were there, it would have been quite impossible for you to have seen anything that was going on in Dorset Street or in any of the turnings off it. So for a moment, my sister lost her nerve and remembered that wicked people sometimes use charming young girls to get into gardens and kidnap babies. Her own baby was in the garden, to say nothing of half a dozen children belonging to neighbors of high degree; they were all in her charge and so—"

"—and so she pushed me out," finished Jody. "But I *was* going to Madame Latour's and I *was* found at the bottom of her staircase."

He frowned. He was sitting forward in a chair, his attitude easy and relaxed. Something in his air, however, told the two women that he was turning something over in his mind, and they waited for him to speak.

"It would be interesting," he said slowly at last, "to know just what happened that morning."

"We know what happened," said Lady Cleeve. "My niece fell down a flight of stone steps and hit her head at the bottom."

Desmond Huntley's eyes, dark and thoughtful, rested on her.

"You know the beginning and you know the end," he pointed out. "But there seems to be rather a gap in between."

"Does it matter?" Jody asked him.

"It would matter to me." His tone was reflective. "You feel satisfied because you've cleared up this business of the goat, but in your place, I think I'd like to go a step or two further and try to plot the course."

"You mean that if she wasn't near Madame Latour's flat, where was she?" asked Lady Cleeve.

"Something like that," he said. "You wouldn't," he asked them, "care to drive round with me to Dorset Court and try to relate time and place?"

Jody stared at him.

"I don't quite understand," she said.

"It's perfectly simple," smiled Desmond. "You know what time you got to Dorset Court that morning. You know what time you were found at the bottom of the stairs. It would be interesting to see how far you could have got in between." He glanced at his watch. "There's time before dinner, and my car fits two and a half. We could go round there now— that is, if you cared to."

He looked at Lady Cleeve, who was doing a little arithmetic. He would take up enough space for two. Two from two and a half . . .

"I won't go, thank you," she said.

He looked at Jody.

"How about it?" he asked.

She hesitated. She had no great wish to go. She had satisfied herself that she had really seen a man and a goat. The fact that seeing them both and talking over the event in a sensible fashion had done nothing to remove her strange sense of fear was something she could think about later.

She heard her aunt's dry tones.

"You'd better go, Jody, and get the thing cleared up if you can."

And get this over-large man removed, her glance added. Nobody had never punished her chair springs as he was doing. But he had been kind to come and settle the matter of the goat, and she owed him something.

"In that cabinet behind you," she told Desmond, "you'll find drinks and glasses. Will you help yourself? For me, and for my niece, sherry."

He walked to the cabinet, and poured drinks, conscious of his hostess's eye upon him. She rose and rearanged the cushions he had flattened, and replaced two ornaments with which he had been fidgeting. Then she reseated herself and watched silently his increasingly clumsy movements at the cocktail cabinet. Under her unblinking regard, Desmond spilled several drops of sherry on the carpet, knocked over a small table and ended by breaking one of the exquisite crystal decanters.

Jody, in pity, left her drink and went into her bedroom to get ready to go out. When she returned to the drawing room, Clarice was picking up pieces of glass and Lady Cleeve and Desmond were eyeing one another coldly from opposite corners of the room.

"Your aunt," he told Jody as he put her into his car, "is rather formidable, if I may say so."

"She doesn't like men very much."

He glanced at her engagement ring.

"And does she give your fiancé the fisheye when he comes to see you?"

Jody smiled.

"He doesn't have to come. I don't live here."

"You don't? Then—"

"I live with my sister at a place called Broome in Sussex. My brother-in-law is the Headmaster of the boys' school there, and my fiancé's the science master."

"And you commute?"

"Yes."

"Wouldn't you rather live nearer London?"

"In winter, perhaps," acknowledged Jody. "This is a nice car," she commented.

"She's fast. If you'd ever let me drive you down to Broome, I could show you what she can do." He grinned. "I brought Betsy to town in the back seat. Incidentally"—he paused at the traffic lights and glanced at Jody—"my sister wants to apologize. She said that the moment you'd gone, she was sorry she'd had a moment's doubt about you. You were too obviously all right to have had sinister intentions—and besides, your story was so lame."

"Why did you follow it up?" Jody asked curiously.

"Because she told me you were the most attractive girl she'd ever seen," he answered calmly.

She found nothing to say to this. There was silence until they reached Dorset Court and Desmond had drawn up before the great block of flats. He walked round to help her out, and together they went toward the rather ornate north entrance. Then Jody halted.

"Not this way," she said.

He looked down at her; she was barely up to his shoulder.

"You remember going in?"

"I don't exactly remember going in, but I know that this wasn't the entrance I was making for."

"And that"—he turned to face her—"that's the first puzzle. You came to see Madame Latour. You arrived punctually—that is, with ample time to get to her flat at the time of the appointment: eleven-thirty. So why do you, having arrived on time, go toward the wrong entrance? Look"—he pointed to the large, clear notices—"it's there for all to read, and you're a sensible girl; you wouldn't walk past a notice as large as that without checking the number you want."

"I didn't have to check the number," Jody told him. "I'd often been to Dorset Court before, giving treatments, and I knew my way around."

"But you didn't know," he insisted. "If you'd known, this is the entrance you would have used, because this is the entrance which leads to her flat. I'll take you there now, and I'll prove to you that you couldn't possibly have seen me or the goat from that side of the block—not unless you were looking through several intervening flats. Come on."

He took her arm and led her toward the short flight of steps that led to the north entrance—and then he felt her resisting.

"I didn't come this way. I'm absolutely certain I didn't," she said.

Something in her voice halted him. He stood looking down at her for a few moments without speaking.

"If all this is bothering you," he said slowly at last, "we'll skip it."

"No. Yes. I don't know," faltered Jody.

"You sounded—a moment or two ago—as though you were frightened."

"I'm not frightened. At least—"

"But you're uneasy?"

"I . . . I don't know."

"When you saw me at the door of your aunt's house, there was fear on your face. Why?"

"I don't know."

He took her hand and led her back to the car and placed her in it. Taking his seat beside her, he made no move to drive away; instead, he turned and faced her and began to speak gently.

"I'm sorry I've upset you," he said. "But I happen to have

a lot of time on my hands, and I was interested in the story my sister told me. It seemed obvious that I must find you and make my sister's apology—but I also wanted to know exactly what lay behind your desire to see the goat. And having found out, it seemed to me that there are one or two loose strings which it would be interesting to tie up. But since we left your aunt's house, you've changed. You've got a scared look in your eyes—and if that's what playing about with loose threads is going to do for you, we'll just cut them and go back and pick up your aunt and go out to dinner somewhere, if you'll both come, and we'll give up this idea of poking into the past. Agreed?"

Jody, opening her mouth to give a heartfelt agreement, found to her dismay that no words came. Instead, she stared at Desmond, and the look in her eyes made him reach out and take her hand in a firm clasp.

"Yes?" he urged.

"No."

The word was out before she could stop it. It hung in the air and she sat staring straight before her and wondering if she had really uttered it. Then she looked at Desmond.

"I'll have to go in there." She nodded toward the luxurious block of apartments. "I'll have to go in—just to get rid of this feeling of fear. I suppose it's like having a swimming accident—if you don't go into the water straightaway and overcome your fear, you're left with it all your life."

"What exactly are you afraid of?"

"I don't know. I only know it's connected—or was connected—with what I saw: you and the goat. When I think of myself falling down the flight of stairs, or of hurting myself, I feel nothing much—just a mild feeling of surprise that it happened to me. But when I see that picture—you pulling the goat, looking back at it, urging it along toward the door . . . then I feel sick with fear. When I saw you standing at the door, the fear came back. Looking at you now, sitting here and talking to you, it seems incredible that the sight of you could have made anybody feel frightened—but I was frightened. I am frightened."

"Of me?"

"No. Of something connected with you."

"And the connection between yourself and myself is in there, inside Dorset Court, and so you're scared to go in."

"Yes. But I . . . I want to go in. If you'd forgive me for

being stupid, and if you'd be patient and take me in and
. . . and let me hang onto you if this panic comes on, I'll"—
her eyes, wide and clear, stared into his—"I'll be grateful to
you as long as I live. You're a stranger, and I've no right to
ask you. I've got a brother-in-law and a fiancé—but they've
both told me rather firmly that there's to be no looking back.
The doctor told them I was being morbid, and they believe
him."

"What's morbid about trying to fill in a missing half-hour
or so?"

"Nothing—I hope. You said you had time to kill. Well, I've
got a ghost to lay. So . . ."

He had taken her other hand; now the two lay in his own,
and he looked down at them.

"See those?" he said. "My vast paws and your absurd little
ones? Hang on—and don't let go."

Then they were out of the car and walking once more toward the building.

"Now," said Desmond, when they had entered the hall,
"pay attention. You say that Madame Latour's on *that* side,
and I—Nancy and I—say she's on *this*. First we'll prove that
the Huntleys are never wrong. Relax, and just go where I go
—and let your mind rest; don't start speculating yet."

They were in the elevator and he had pressed the first-
floor button.

"It's only one flight," he said, "but we're taking the elevator because you, carrying your beauty equipment, would
probably have taken it." He ushered her out of the elevator.
"Now we're on Madame Latour's floor—and here, at the end
of this little corridor—come and look—is Madame Latour's
flat. There."

He had stopped before a door. Jody stared at the number
upon it, and opened her mouth to speak. Desmond put up a
hand.

"Don't say anything yet," he ordered. "Come here. You
see where you are? You're standing in a corridor a few yards
long and there's one flat and one flat only before you: Madame Latour's. There are eighteen elevators in this block; I
know, because in my time I've used pretty well all of them.
You come out of the elevators and you can turn three ways:
along the main corridor, along a secondary corridor, or, in
the case of corner flats, along a short corridor that leads only
to the corner flats. Madame Latour's is a corner flat, as you

see. And in the corridor—observe—is one window and one window only. Look out of it and what do you see?"

Jody looked out.

"You see?" he asked. "Not a sign of Waverley Mews."

She turned and looked up at him.

"I didn't need to look," she said.

"Good. Then we're a step forward."

"No. We're a step back," said Jody. "Because I was never here."

"You can remember?"

"No. But this flat is Number Seven."

"You said Madame Latour's."

"I know I did. But I must have made a mistake, because I thought her flat was number . . .'" She stopped, and fear flickered in her eyes. "I've . . . I've forgotten."

His voice was level.

"It would be easy to check, wouldn't it? You must have her letter—or did she telephone and ask for an appointment?"

"She wrote. And I must have copied the number wrongly into my appointment book."

"And where's the appointment book?"

"At the office."

"Which means that—this being Friday—we can't do anything until Monday?"

"I could get into the office and get to my desk—if you thought it was important."

"If we're going to clear this up, it's important to know which number you went to. Come on back to the car; you can direct me to your office."

The caretaker let them in, and Jody led Desmond to the desk she used. She opened a drawer and took from it her notebook. Desmond watched her as she found the entry.

"Got it?" he asked.

"Yes." She raised puzzled eyes to his. "I've written down Number Four."

"We all make mistakes."

"Yes. But . . . I've worked here for over two years," she said slowly, "and this is the first time I've ever got an address wrong."

"Where's the letter from Madame Latour?"

She walked to a filing cabinet, drew out a file, found a letter and stood staring at it.

"Well?" he asked.

"It . . . it *is* Number Four!"

He came over and took the letter from her and looked at it—and then she heard him laugh.

"Seven," he said.

"That's a four!"

"It's like a four, but it isn't a four. Because why? Because Madame Latour is a Frenchwoman, and the French, for reasons of their own, insist on making ones look like sevens—they put a little dash through them. Then, just to make it more difficult, they make sevens look like fours. When they use a pen like Madame Latour's, the whole thing gets out of hand."

She was staring at him.

"And so . . . so that's why . . ."

"That's why," he said. "And this time we really are a step forward. Come on."

"Come on where to?"

"Back to Dorset Court. This time, we're going to Number Four, and I think we shall prove three things: one, that it's a corner flat, at the end of a short corridor; two, that from the window of the corridor, you had, as you waited for somebody to open the door, a clear view of my sister's front door, and you would have had a grandstand view of me trying to get the goat along to its new home. Three . . . well, number three is only conjecture, but it would explain a lot of things. If the door opened and you saw something that frightened you . . ." He paused and looked down at her, trying to weigh up her reactions. "You don't remember *anything?*"

"Nothing."

"Were you found at the bottom of Madame Latour's stairs?"

"No. I fell down the flight of stairs near Number Four. But when they told me where they found me—"

"—you took it for granted that Number Four was Madame Latour's flat. I see. Well, let's go."

The drove to Dorset Court once more, and this time Desmond led her to the south entrance. They went up a single flight in the elevator and then they got out and found themselves in a corridor which corresponded in every detail to that leading to Madame Latour's apartment. Only the view was different. From the window, as Desmond had told her, she could see clearly the quiet little road, the trim houses, the yellow door.

"You see?" came Desmond's voice quietly. "You'd ring the bell, and as you waited for somebody to answer it, you'd turn naturally to look out of the window. And you'd see me trying to get Betsy along. And after that . . . well, what? If the door opened and something frightened you, wouldn't you turn and run back along this corridor and make for the stairs? People in a panic don't stand and wait for elevators. You get to the stairs, and you go down them faster than you mean to, and they find you at the bottom, unconscious."

"But—"

"Wait a minute. All we have to do now is to ring the bell of Number Four and see whether Frankenstein answers the door. If he doesn't, and if somebody normal-looking answers it, we merely ask whether you called on them on the morning of—what date was it?"

"Tuesday the fifteenth."

"Well, let's ring the bell and start asking questions."

The questions were soon answered. Number Four was empty. A new tenant was shortly to move in.

When, inquired Desmond at the reception desk on the ground floor, had the previous tenants left?

Some reference to ledgers was necessary; then the clerk remembered that the previous tenants, a Mr. and Mrs. Grierson, had left in something of a hurry. They had been called away urgently, he said, and had left the building at about one o'clock, less than an hour after Mrs. Grierson had come down to tell him that they were leaving. He had sent upstairs for their luggage. Mrs. Grierson had left in a taxi; Mr. Grierson, she said, had gone on ahead to his bank. Their address—Yes, here it was. Very difficult to pronounce; somewhere in Kenya.

"What date did they leave?" asked Desmond.

The clerk consulted the ledger once more, and Jody and Desmond waited. Then the man looked up.

"The tenants left," he said, "on the morning of Tuesday the fifteenth."

# CHAPTER
## 5

IT WAS, ARGUED DESMOND, taking Jody's arm and moving her out of earshot of the clerk, it was pure coincidence. People, he pointed out, didn't take these furnished apartments forever. Flat-dwellers were birds of passage, who stayed three months, six months, perhaps a year. Only people who bought apartments stayed in them. He couldn't, come to think of it, cite a single instance of any friends of his staying in a furnished flat longer than a year. They moved in, they moved out. Inagain, outagain, awayagain, Finnegan, that's who they were.

To this monologue Jody listened with a faint smile. At the end of it, she had only one brief question.

"Who's frightened now?" she asked.

He stared at her.

"I tell you, it's pure coincidence," he repeated. "Are you going to try and build something sinister out of a coincidence?"

"The Griersons," she reminded him, "came to the clerk at noon on the fifteenth and asked him to send up for their luggage. They left by taxi. The only address they gave, on coming or going, was a fictitious-sounding one in Kenya. So that half an hour after I saw them—because why wouldn't I see them?—I went to their flat and I must have rung the doorbell—they pack up and vanish."

"Pure coincidence."

"Which was the coincidence?" she asked. "The coincidence of my going to see them about an hour before they left, or the coincidence of my being found at the bottom of their stairs about an hour before they left? Or the fact that I was left with a feeling of panic after seeing them? Because you know something? I'm certain that I did see them."

"I've told you what you could have done. You go to the wrong flat. You ring the bell. This Grierson answers it, sees a

49

pretty girl on his doorstep and says or does something to frighten you. Being a sensible girl, you don't wait to be the fly in the spider's parlor; you run for it. He feels fairly certain that you'll lodge a complaint downstairs, so he alerts his wife and they pack up and push off. Not because they fear your complaint in itself but because the fellow was probably one of the maniacs you read about who'd been up for similar offenses before. He doesn't want more trouble, so he tells his wife to pack, and they vanish. Why won't you accept that as a sound reconstruction?"

"I'll have to," said Jody, with a touch of her aunt's dryness. "There's no way of proving anything."

Or, it seemed, of getting any further information. The clerk had summoned an underling, placed him in charge and gone off duty. The hall was empty; the very air seemed charged with indifference.

Jody moved away from the counter.

"Investigation over," she told Desmond. "But"—she gave him a smile that made his head reel—"thank you all the same."

"I'm sorry. I hoped it would kill that bogey."

Jody stopped and swung round to face him.

"Oh—but it *has!*"

"It *has?*" he echoed. "But—"

She laughed at his bewilderment, and walked to the car, and he fell into step beside her.

"You mean you're not frightened any more?" he asked.

"I don't know. Perhaps I am," she said. "But if the fear's still there, then fear is a much less strong emotion than curiosity. You've removed panic and left me with a frustrated feeling—like the girl reporter who didn't get her scoop."

He put her into the car and then took the wheel.

"I'm curious, too," he said, "but we seem to be the only ones in that building who wanted to hear anything more about the Griersons. They—"

He stopped. A man had come down the steps of the main entrance and was hurrying toward the car, clearly with the object of speaking to them. Desmond, who had switched on the engine, switched it off again and waited, and the man— short, stout and bald-headed—came to a breathless stop beside the car.

"Ah—I'm not too late," he said. "The reception clerk told

me that you had been making inquiries about Mr. and Mrs. Grierson."

"Yes," said Desmond. "Has he remembered something?"

"He went off duty and happened to see me—I am Mr. Kennedy, the Reception Manager—and he mentioned that a young lady and gentleman had been asking about Mr. and Mrs. Grierson. So I came out to ask whether you were by any chance friends of theirs."

"We didn't even know their names," explained Desmond, "until we checked up on Apartment Number Four. This lady"—he indicated Jody—"had a slight accident on the morning the Griersons left, and doesn't remember much about what happened—but we thought that she might have gone by mistake to Number Four. Since the Griersons have left, there doesn't seem much hope of clearing up the point."

"I see." Mr. Kennedy stared at them out of keen, hard, intelligent little black eyes. "I'm sorry we haven't been able to help you. Mr. and Mrs. Grierson left very abruptly."

"So we gathered just now," said Desmond. "Leaving a Kenya address."

"That is so. We knew very little about them," said Mr. Kennedy. "In fact"—he spread fat, white hands—"in fact, I would not have come out here to see you if I had not been able to add one small item of information to the little the clerk gave you."

"What is it?" asked Jody.

"It doesn't amount to much," confessed Mr. Kennedy, "but if you ever chanced to come upon Mr. and Mrs. Grierson, or friends of theirs, you might be helped by knowing that Mrs. Grierson's name is Laurie."

"Laurie's surely his name?" said Desmond. "It isn't a woman's name."

"So I thought! So I thought," said Mr. Kennedy. "But there was no mistake. I do not work at the reception counter, but sometimes I spend a few moments there—to ask something, to check something. By the merest chance, I happened to be there when Mrs. Grierson came in with a friend —a lady friend. I did not know Mrs. Grierson by sight, but when I looked up and saw her, I was struck by her looks. She is young—not more than thirty, I would say—and remarkably handsome; she had naturally fair hair. She came to the counter to ask a question about train times, and I heard her friend address her as Laurie."

There was a pause.

"Well, that ought to help," said Desmond drily. "She's a blonde and they call her Laurie. Is Mr. Grierson a blond too?"

"That," said Mr. Kennedy, "I cannot tell you. The apartment was taken by Mrs. Grierson, for—she said—her husband and herself. She lived, for the most part, alone—but she entertained a great deal, and from time to time"—he glanced apologetically at Jody—"there were evidences that somebody had stayed in the apartment for a night or two. But he—if it was a he, and if it was Mr. Grierson—came with other guests, and left early in the morning, and no one on the staff can state who the elusive Mr. Grierson was, or what he looked like. All this, of course, was known to the Reception Department; we did not intend to renew the lease when it came to an end."

"She was blonde, and she was called Laurie, and any one of several visiting gentlemen could have been her husband—right?" asked Desmond.

"It doesn't sound much," said Mr. Kennedy regretfully, "but it may help you. I hope it does."

There was an odd note in his voice, and Jody stared at him.

"Are you anxious to find them too?" she asked.

All expression drained out of the shoe-button eyes.

"Anxious? Perhaps. I would find it interesting," said Mr. Kennedy, "to discover why there was a small trace of blood on the drawing-room carpet of Number Four."

There was another pause, this time a long one.

"If there was blood around," asked Desmond levelly at last, "why didn't you call in the police?"

Mr. Kennedy smiled—a mirthless smile.

"We only call in the police," he said, "when we are compelled to. We do not call them in for nothing."

"*Nothing?*" echoed Jody. "Do you call bloodstains nothing?"

Mr. Kennedy seemed to hesitate.

"I have told you this," he said slowly at last, "because I think that you have reasons for the inquiries that you are making about Mr. and Mrs. Grierson. I have placed in your hands all the information we possess—and I trust that you will use it with discretion."

He gave a slight bow, and without further speech turned

and walked away. They saw him go up the steps, awkward but agile; then he was swallowed up by the building.

They sat in silence for a moment, and then Desmond spoke thoughtfully.

"Well, what exactly do you make of all that?" he asked.

Jody folded her hands in her lap.

"I don't have to make anything of it," she said calmly. "You brought me here because you were going to clear everything up."

"I brought you here because I didn't want you to go on being afraid."

"Then you should have stopped our fat friend before he told us about the blood on the carpet. Obviously, it was my blood. Obviously, Mr. Grierson dragged me into the drawing room—while Laurie was downstairs checking up on more trains—and attacked me. Then I escaped—and fell downstairs. When I recovered, I remembered the man and the goat, and naturally thought that the goat had butted me down the stairs—and all my life, when I see a goat, or a red-haired man, I shall give a loud scream and faint."

Her summing-up came to an end, and she eyed him, waiting for his comments. He grinned at her.

"All right," he said. "I brought you here, and it was a washout. Where do we go now?"

"We follow the yellow brick road."

"The what?"

"The yellow brick road."

"And where does that lead us?" he wanted to know.

"Nobody knows. But there's supposed to be a wizard at the end of it, and he might be able to tell us something."

"And along this yellow brick road, we find Laurie?"

"We might."

Desmond started the engine and the car moved smoothly out into the road.

"We can rule out Kenya," he said. "That's no place for hideouts. The place that anybody would hide in, after leaving patches of blood on carpets, is right here in the heart of London."

"That makes it easy for us," remarked Jody. "A mere eight million or so—and only about a million of them can be natural blondes."

"But not all of them can be called Laurie." Desmond turned to smile at her, missed a bus by inches and gave his attention to the road once more. "Anyhow, I've enjoyed it and I hope you'll let me go on trying to work something out."

"You said you had time on your hands. But I'm afraid," said Jody, "that I haven't. I do two jobs—one here in London, and the other at home in Broome."

"Nancy's husband has a cottage in Sussex and is always trying to induce her to go and spend a few weeks in it," Desmond told her. "If she did, I could see something of you —and try to solve one more mystery."

"What mystery?" she asked.

"Whether your fiancé knows what a prize he's drawn. Do you think," he went on without pause, "that your aunt would come out to dinner with us?"

"I'm afraid not."

"And there isn't the least hope, I suppose, that she'll ask me to stay to dinner with her?"

"I'm afraid not."

He brought the car to a halt outside her aunt's house and turned to look at her.

"When do I see you again?" he asked. "Something tells me you regard this parting as final; I can see it in your eyes, which at this moment look remarkably like your aunt's."

"I'm sorry," said Jody, "but—"

"Look." His tone was reasonable. "You can't just throw me out of your life. I don't want to butt into anything, or to upset your fiancé or your family by hanging round you, but couldn't you explain to them that we're trying to find out how you got hurt that morning? They must want to know what happened."

"They don't. They feel that the whole thing ought to be forgotten as soon as possible."

"Then they're wrong. The more you know, the less you fear. We've just proved it. We found a clue—don't you want to follow it up?"

"I don't think there's the smallest hope of ever finding the Griersons, if that's what you mean."

"Don't you want to try?"

She hesitated.

"How could we begin?" she asked at last. "I'm busy all day and busy every evening. You're on leave and you ought to be making the most of it having fun."

"This is fun. What about that yellow brick road you talked about?"

She turned to the door, and he came round to help her out of the car and stood looking down at her, waiting for her answer.

"I'm sorry," she said. "I'm grateful—more grateful than I can say, but . . ."

"No detective work?"

"I'm afraid not."

"And that means that you and Betsy and I were brought together for nothing?" He was in the car once more, and he switched on the engine. "You think Fate takes all that trouble—for nothing?"

"Goodbye," said Jody.

"Nonsense," said Desmond Huntley, and drove away.

# CHAPTER
# 6

JODY GAVE HER AUNT a full account of what had happened, telling the story in serial form as they went from the drawing room to the dining room and then, dinner over, back to the drawing room once more. At the end of the story, Lady Cleeve sat silent and thoughtful, pouring out the coffee and turning over the new developments in her mind.

"And where does all this get you?" she inquired at last.

"Nowhere," said Jody. "Except that I know a bit more of what happened that morning."

"Do you think that you ran toward the stairs and fell down them?"

"I can't really see myself doing it," said Jody. "I work with and for women, and they sometimes have husbands, and the husbands sometimes get troublesome—but I've never yet had to run."

Her aunt looked at her thoughtfully.

"It's very hard," she said, "to see you as the heroine of a melodrama."

"Not the heroine—the victim," corrected Jody.

"Well, you're still miscast. You're not at all the kind of girl who fits into anything spectacular, you know. All your life, you've been given a choice between the exciting and the humdrum, and always—"

"The humdrum. I know. I like things that way: quiet, peaceful, going along without upheavals."

"You could have lived here with me, and you elected to go down to Estelle's and turn yourself into a *hausfrau*. You could have met some extremely eligible men in town, but you preferred to accept the first science master who proposed to you. And there," she ended, "is where I think the real trouble lies."

"I don't understand."

"Well, let me enlighten you. Do you know that you've

never really been yourself—what I call yourself—since you became engaged? I told you at the time that it was a mistake, and I think you feel—deep down—that you acted in too much of a hurry. But you refuse to acknowledge to yourself that it's a mistake, and because you won't face it, it's beginning to give you this kind of psychological trouble."

"That's nonsense, Aunt Essie."

"Why is it nonsnse? For four years, you've been leading a completely unnatural life—that is, you've been living Estelle's life, and her husband's life, and not your own. And now you've got engaged to a man who won't—I'm quite certain—make you happy."

"Charles is all right."

"Who said he wasn't? He'll make a very good husband for a mermaid or a sea nymph, because he'll always be near sea water. If you marry him, you'll spend your life sitting on the quay at Marcove with his lunch or his dinner in a little basket, waiting for him to bring his boat into harbor." She paused. "These are the summer holidays—how much time is he spending with you?"

"He has to give a lot of extra lessons. He—"

"If I thought he was giving them in order to make things more comfortable for you when you marry, I should be very happy. But I'm worried because all his plans for the future seem to be for himself. Does he talk about a home for you when you marry? No. All he wants is a bigger and better boat."

"But Aunt Essie, you—"

"I don't care for men—is that what you were going to say? Well, it's true—but I realize that women can't have children without their cooperation, and I would like you to have children. I'd like to see you with one or two pretty little girls—but if you marry Charles, you'll produce nothing but a succession of seamen."

"I like sailing. I like going sailing with him."

"When you're married to him, you'll have as much of it as you want. It won't work, Jody. He's a man with no desire for a settled home—and you're a girl who needs one. The life he's offering you isn't the life you want, and I think that, subconsciously, you know it. But because you refuse to face it, you're running into trouble of the psychological kind."

"I didn't imagine all this, Aunt Essie. It *happened*."

"But you can't shake it off. You're weaving mysteries out of it."

"I'm not weaving them," said Jody mildly. "They wuz wove."

"Then don't do any more weaving. Leave things as they are, and forget this mysterious woman called Laurie. She, and people like her, are the kind of persons to stay away from. Remember that whatever happened that morning, you're safe and well now. Stay that way."

"It would have been nice to know exactly what did happen."

Lady Cleeve made no answer. She was thinking of Desmond Huntley. He and Jody had gone out as strangers, and in less than an hour had seemed to have got onto easy, friendly terms. On his side, indeed, the terms sounded something more than friendly. It was easy to fall in love with Jody, she mused—but it wouldn't get him anywhere. Jody was the faithful kind; she had chosen her science master and she would stick to him. It was a pity. She admitted to herself that Charles Vaughan had his attractions; his black hair, tanned face and vividly blue eyes gave him good looks of an unusually arresting type; his touchy disposition and irritable temper seemed to have little effect on the calm Jody. He was attractive—but she was convinced that the chief reason for his success had been that strongest of all aids: propinquity. They had met almost daily; the school and his long friendship with Michael drew them together. Everything had been in Charles Vaughan's favor; nothing had appeared to check his smooth and easy advance. Nothing—and nobody.

Until now.

Lady Cleeve stared at her mental picture of the six-feet-three Lieutenant-Commander. It was difficult to reduce him to the proportions of a fly-in-the-ointment, but perhaps . . .

"If you take my advice," she said, "you'll keep this evening's little adventure to yourself."

"I won't tell Estelle or Michael, but I'll have to tell Charles."

"If you do, you'll make him angry—and you'll worry him. Haven't they all warned you to forget the whole affair?"

"Yes, but this is a new development."

"And if you tell them about it, you'll start all the arguments again. If you take my advice, you'll keep it entirely between yourself and Commander Huntley."

She was amazed at her own subtlety. There was nothing so cozy as a secret shared. This massive young naval man, with his rugged look, his quiet, relaxed, easy manner, was the kind of husband she had sketched in her mind for Jody. This Huntley could offer a magnificent physique, an easygoing way that seemed to conceal hidden power, eyes like an antelope's, and a general shaggy-dog appeal. A little competition might wake Charles Vaughan up. Soon, perhaps, there would be two yachtsmen coming into Marcove with eyes searching the shore for Jody's small figure. It was a situation which met with her entire approval.

She looked up to find Jody's eyes on her.

"You don't like Charles much, do you, Aunt Essie?"

This was thought-reading indeed. Lady Cleeve sat up straighter.

"I daresay he'll make an average husband," she conceded.

"Was Uncle Bruce a good husband?" asked Jody.

Lady Cleeve considered.

"I think so," she said at last. "I daresay most women would have thought so. But when I lunched with him today, I was very glad that I could leave him and come back here—alone. Why is it that so many people dread living alone?"

"People like people, that's why."

"Round them incessantly, day and night?"

"Especially night."

"Nobody who examined my bookshelves could say I lived alone," said Lady Cleeve. "All those brilliant men and women—bound in calf." She gave a sign of contentment. "Jody, I'm a happy woman—but I suppose I'm a selfish one."

"I don't think you're at all selfish."

"Michael seems to think I am. He said so, with emphasis, only yesterday."

"Michael?" Jody stared at her aunt in astonishment. "You saw him yesterday? I thought—"

"You thought we had more or less agreed to stay away from one another. So did I. But he came here yesterday."

"Why?"

"To borrow money."

There was a pause.

"And did you . . ."

"I refused."

"I . . . I see," said Jody.

"I don't think you do. Did you know that he had tried to borrow money from Charles?"

"Yes. They . . . they had a quarrel about it."

"Then that makes two quarrels. I told Michael exactly what I thought of him. I enjoyed it—but he didn't."

"He isn't as bad as you make out, Aunt Essie."

"I've never accused him of badness, my dear Jody. I merely pointed out to him that the very day Estelle got her money, at twenty-five, it went into the school."

"Why shouldn't it? It's her life as well as his."

"That may be, and I wasn't able to stop her—but I can and will refuse to lend him any of my money. And in a month or two, you'll be twenty-five and the trustees will hand you over your capital, and Michael will be after it. But I'm glad to see that Charles feels as I do—that enough has been poured into the school. Drink up your coffee, and I'll ring for Clarice. Don't tell Estelle that Michael came to see me—and don't tell any of them that you went to Dorset Court to-night."

Keeping Estelle and Michael in ignorance, Jody felt, was wise. It was also, she found when she returned to Broome on Saturday morning, easy, for both were out for the day.

She packed a basket of food and went across to Miss Bishop's cottage to see if she could beg a lift to Marcove; Miss Bishop owned a trim little car and liked to drive to the Cove, park the car near the cliff path and go for a brisk walk along the cliffs or along the beach. There was no sign of her or the car, however, and Jody concluded that she was out. The Professor's car—a high, black, ancient affair with a noble but 1912 engine—stood outside his cottage, but Jody did not ask for a lift in it. She had only once been driven by the Professor: it had been a hazardous experience; one to remember but not to repeat. She marveled each time he reappeared, safe and sound, from the expeditions he made once a month to his Conservatoire in Yorkshire; some special Providence, she thought, must protect him. She had another reason for not asking him to drive her to Marcove; she knew that he hated and feared the sea and refused to take his car along the narrow, dizzy lane that cut across the cliffs above the little harbor.

She decided that she would walk. The shortcut was rough and in parts precipitous, but it took two miles off the distance, and—like most of the boys and masters—she knew every inch of it.

She enjoyed the walk; the wind was high, but it was also warm. When she reached Marcove, she stood on the cliff-top and looked down at the tiny harbor below. *Gazelle* was not there. The school's two dinghies bobbed between two fishing boats; on *Ballerina's* deck she could see the Major, and although she could not hear him, she knew that he was singing, for he sang most of the time, and sang songs that were not at all like the sober strains he played in Estelle's drawing room. Not far from where Jody stood was his windblown cottage, its doors and windows usually open to the breeze but now locked for the period of his residence in the school cottage. Halfway between cliff and harbor perched the shack known as the Tar Barrel, willing to sell mild drinks to thirty schoolboys and licensed to sell something stronger to thirty fishermen.

Jody walked down to the harbor, greeting on her way the group of customers seated on a bench in the sunshine; all were known to her, for strangers seldom came to Marcove. Approach from the land side was difficult, and accommodation in the harbor limited. Only a few fishermen from Broome kept their boats there; the others found Newhaven a more convenient harbor.

Looking out to sea, Jody saw *Gazelle* coming in, and stood watching her dance her way to the shore. She could see Charles busy with the ropes, and understood how stifling he found the long hours spent in classrooms. This was his element. The sea was white-flecked, the water almost emerald. Now and then a shower of spray would break against the harbor wall and fall back with a hiss, like an angry sea creature struggling to leap onto the land. Close to the shore were the fishing boats, dipping and plunging; beyond them sailed other craft, graceful and white-sailed. In the distance, Jody could see the mail steamer, Dieppe-bound, emerging from Newhaven and dipping gracefully as if in farewell to the coast of England.

The Major, from *Ballerina's* deck, turned a professional glance on the rapidly approaching *Gazelle*.

"You should be out with him, Jody," he said. "Wonderful day for a sail. Take you myself, if you'll come. 'As we go rolling, over the rolling, over the rolling sea'" he caroled.

Jody looked at him with a smile. She had never, she thought, met a Jack-of-all-trades until the Major had come to Broome. Once a soldier, now a first-class sailor. A good musician, an expert gardener, a handy carpenter. He seemed to have traveled everywhere and seen everything, and he was as adaptable as a chameleon; neat and serious in Estelle's drawing room, playing the Professor's intricate compositions, and now in patched blue trousers and faded blue shirt, gay and carefree and filling the air with music-hall memories.

> "Twas a June afternoon, and a sentimental coon
> Stood alone in the shadow of the trees."

he sang, and broke off to address Jody once more. "Missed you after the practice the other night."

"I had to go up to town."

"Ha. You didn't fall down any more flights of stairs?"

"No."

"What I said when they told me about it," said the Major, busily polishing brass, "was: Why choose stone staircases? You could have practiced a fall or two down a wooden flight." He took a step backwards to blink admiringly at the rail twinkling in the sunshine. "That is, if you really did fall," he ended.

She looked at him.

"You think someone pushed me?"

The Major looked shocked.

"Who'd push a pretty girl like you? No.

> "'All along the rails, oh what a lively gang,
> Shouting out the chorus, to everyone we sang.
> We laughed, we chaffed, we—'

"No, not pushed. But I said to myself when I heard about it: Funny thing that; seen scores of people come scores of croppers down scores of flights of stairs, but never saw one end up with a bump on the back of the head. Never. Sprained arm, yes; broken leg, maybe; scraped elbow, perhaps; allover bruises, certainly. You have any bruises?"

Jody hesitated, and depression crept over her. He was taking the sunshine out of the day.

"No," she said at last.

"Don't like talking about it?" he asked.

> " 'Has anybody here seen Kelly?
> Kelly from the Isle of—'

"Your folks don't like talking about it either. I said a word or two to the Headmaster, and he bally near blew my head off. Can't see why, I must say. Subject taboo?"

"The doctor told him that it would be better if I forgot the whole thing."

"I see. Don't agree with him, but that's neither here nor there; not my business.

> " 'Last night the night-in-gale woke me
> Last night when all was still.'

"All I thought—There I go again."

"All you thought—?"

"Well, who said you fell downstairs? Anybody see you go down?"

"No."

"A chap comes to mend the elevator and sees you lying at the foot of the stairs and says to himself: 'Hello, young lady fallen downstairs.' And he tells that to the management and they take it for a fact. Myself, I think you didn't fall down those stairs. Myself, I think you did a nice little maidenly swoon at the bottom of them and in falling, gave your head a whang on the concrete. That way, no bumps, no bruises, no fractures. See what I mean?"

"Yes."

"Don't mind my bringing it up?"

"No. No, you're very kind."

"Kind?" The Major seemed to give the adjective his consideration. "Kind? Well, no; I was just trying to get the thing straight in my my own mind. I don't believe all I'm told, not by a long chalk. Do you?"

"As a rule."

"Great mistake.

> " 'Shine little glow-worm, glimm-er,
> Shine little glow-worm, glimm-er
> Lead us lest too far we wander
> Love's sweet—'

"Here's your young man coming in. But don't you go telling him I've touched on the forbidden topic. He's like the Headmaster: liable to blow up without notice."

She turned to watch Charles coming in, but her mind was full of the Major's theory. If he was right, if she had fainted before going up the stairs, the Griersons—Laurie and her husband—could be ruled out. There was nothing to show that she had ever been to their apartment. There was no reason to suppose that her accident had any connection with their hurried departure from Dorset Court. Mr. Kennedy's action in coming out to Desmond Huntley's car could have been nothing more than the officiousness of an over-zealous employee.

A feeling of humiliation crept over her. Looking at last night's events in this clear air, and with the Major's sensible words in her ears, Mr. Kennedy and his mysterious hints and his talk of blood and blondes seemed so ridiculous, so ludicrous, that she felt herself growing hot with shame for having taken them for a moment seriously.

She drew a deep breath, and inwardly blessed the Major for having saved her from making a fool of herself. Clean air, cliffs, and the dancing Channel—all about her, as she stood, were evidences of sane, healthy living—and melodrama, and Mr. Kennedy could be put into their proper perspective.

She stepped aboard *Gazelle*. Charles tilted her chin and dropped a light kiss on her mouth.

"Long time no see," he said. "Why did you stay up in town last night?"

What had she been about to say before the Major's timely remarks brought her back to her senses? *Well, I met the man with the goat, and he thinks that Mr. Grierson chased me down the stairs, and then he and his wife—she's a natural blonde and awfully attractive—packed up and fled to Kenya, leaving blood on the drawing-room carpet. . . .*

She felt the hot color in her cheeks.

"I stayed to dinner with Aunt Essie," she said.

"Clear soup, steamed sole and coffee."

"Quite right."

"That woman . . . What's in the basket?" he broke off to ask.

"What did you want in the basket?"

"Cold beef sandwiches with plenty of mustard; a chicken

bone to chew on; a hunk of cheese, Stilton for preference, and any fruit that's going, cherries for choice."

"I read your mind."

"Then while you unpack it and lay it out, I'll pop up to the Tar Barrel and bring down a couple of beers. No, I won't; we'll have that bottle of wine we brought down last week and didn't drink."

He settled Jody in the sunshine on a part of the deck out of sight of both the Tar Barrel and the Major; she spread out the food and he fetched the wine and poured it out. On a day like this, with a picnic lunch between them, they could almost enjoy the Major's unceasing songs.

When they had eaten, Charles stretched himself along the deck and rested his head on Jody's lap and gave a sigh of pleasure.

"This is the life—isn't it?"

"Does it bring in any money?"

"This time next year, we'll be living on yours. Do you love me?"

She smiled down at him.

"I think so. Couldn't we live on your money too?"

"We'll be doing that—quite literally. I'm buying *Ballerina*."

"You're . . . you're *what?*" asked Jody in astonishment.

"Buying *Ballerina*. At least, I think so. The Major wants to sell her. He knows I've always had my eye on her."

"Have you—"

"—come to a definite agreement? No. But I'm taking her across to Saint-Malo the day after tomorrow; trial trip. If I like the way she behaves, I'll buy her."

"Has he fixed a price?"

"Not yet. He's taking *Gazelle* in part exchange."

"There are other boats. Won't you wait and—"

"I've liked *Ballerina* from the first moment I saw her. I'd like to buy her, and then we could get married and live on her for the rest of the summer."

Jody, examining this proposal, felt that it lacked something, both in matter and in manner. For a moment she hovered on the brink of protest, and then decided to let the sentence go unchallenged. In the silence that followed, she recalled some of her brother-in-law's more high-handed actions and wondered whether she and Estelle were too easygoing; they both, she reflected, let their men get away with a great deal.

She transferred Charles's head from her lap to a cushion, and got up. In the calm, unfussy, casual manner that was one of her charms, she filled a bowl with water, washed the glasses and the cutlery and then, with a fresh supply of water, began to wash two of Charles's shirts. He watched her through drowsy, half-shut eyes as she wrung them out and hung them on an improvised line.

"That's something you don't have to do at your aunt's house," he commented.

"She doesn't wear shirts."

"Sitting in that house of hers always gives me the feeling that I'd like to get up and kick everything in it to pieces. It all looks too . . . it looks unnatural. It's too good to be true. It's lifeless. It's cardboard."

"Expensive cardboard," commented Jody, drying her hands. "You sound like Michael—he called Aunt Essie a queen bee."

"Queen bee? Not your Aunt Essie. A queen bee has at least one use for males. Come and sit down. I want to kiss you."

He drew her down beside him and put his arms round her, and as their lips met, Jody wondered what he would say if she told him what had happened last night at the little cardboard house. She was glad that he did not know.

"One day," he said musingly, "I'll reward you for washing my shirts."

She took a strand of his thick black hair and twisted it into a peak.

"You mean I'll have my carriage and pair?"

"You'll have more than I'm giving you now. One day we'll get away from classrooms and kitchens, and—"

"—out to sea?"

"Why not? Wouldn't you like to live on *Ballerina*?"

"Would there be room for the children?"

"I suppose so. I hadn't," he admitted, "thought of the children."

"Then start thinking."

He peered up at her.

"You mean you want to produce a brood of infants?"

"A quartette. Don't you want a family?"

"Dunno. Babies falling over themselves all over the deck?"

"It's more than a possibility, once we're married."

He fell into a reverie, and she listened to the snatches of

song coming from *Ballerina*, looked down at him and wondered what sort of a father he would make. Michael, in her
opinion often an unsatisfactory husband, was an exemplary
father; perhaps Charles would be the same.

"Let's sail," he said suddenly. "That blasted singing's getting on my nerves."

"So long as we get back early," said Jody. "I want to be
home about six."

He stared at her, his expression one of growing irritation.
"What for?"

"Estelle and Michael and Fenella were out for the day—
I'd like to have a nice dinner waiting for them."

Charles said nothing. They had fought this battle before,
and he had lost. Sitting hunched against the railing, he took
a package of cigarettes from his pocket and lit one.

"What," he inquired coldly after a time, "is Estelle going
to do when you marry me?"

"Get her own dinner," said Jody tranquilly. "But tonight
I'm going to get it, and you're going to eat it."

"The hell I am. What's come over Mike?" Charles's brooding glance was on a friendly gull perched on the mast. "Ten
years ago he was a man you could talk to like an adult.
Today—"

"He thinks you've changed too."

"Perhaps I have. Perhaps I know now what I only suspected ten years ago—that I've got to get out of teaching
and into a job that keeps me out of doors. When Mike
bought the school, I was glad to join the staff, but I never
had the smallest intention of becoming a partner. Which is a
pity, because if I'd agreed to become a partner, I would
have seen to it that the school was run on sound academic
lines, with proper attention paid to examination results and
no attention whatsoever paid to parents, however stinking
with money." He twisted round to stare at Jody. "You know
something? Mike's stopped thinking of study at all; all he
concentrates on nowadays is how he can slam yet another
five or ten pounds onto the fees. The school's lost its reputa-
tion for scholarship and gained one of snobbery. There's a
waiting list three yards long—of boys? No, of parents, mostly
mammas, waiting to tell their friends that little so-and-so has
got into Broome. If I wanted to buy half a school, I wouldn't
buy this one, and that's what I told Mike."

"You told him that before."

"And if I did consider it," went on Charles, unheeding, "I'd turn it down because the one thing I'm aiming to do is get you out of here. You've spent enough time running Mike's house for him."

"If I hadn't wanted to run the house, do you think I would have done it for so long?"

"Yes, I do. I think you're the self-sacrificing type."

"Then you're wrong. If I'd thought it silly to try and keep the house as it is, I would have told Estelle so, and persuaded her to modernize it. I—"

"Yes, but—"

"Listen," said Jody firmly. "I've told you this before, but you've never believed me. I *like* the house as it is. I *like* working in it."

"That's rubbish. You—"

"All over the country," said Jody, "houses like Broome Hall are being thrown to the dogs. Too large, too cold, too old, too difficult to run. Let's get out, everybody says; let's get out and live in a nice little new box with central heating and mod. cons. Old beams? Beautiful ceilings, magnificent staircases, paneling, proportions, period? Nice to look at, but impossible, my dear, to live in; let's get out and be comfortable. So they get out."

"And damned sensible, too."

"But I think Estelle was right to want to . . . to want to live in beauty." She looked at Charles, her eyes wide and thoughtful. "There's so little nowadays. People are all boxed up in neat little compartments."

"That house at Broome was built in the old slave days. It—"

"I know. That's one reason I like it so much. It's got ghosts. Ghosts of beautiful women with the hems of their gowns trailing down the lovely stairs. Ghosts banqueting in the magnificent dining room. Ghosts in the kitchen—cooks, scullions, serving men. Ghosts in the minstrels' gallery; every time I walk along it, I hear the sound of lutes."

His black eyebrows went up.

"Fanciful! I wouldn't have suspected it."

"Yes, you would," she said. "When I said I'd seen a man and a goat, you said—"

"That was entirely different." The amused note had gone from his voice, and he spoke irritably. "Conjuring up pretty pictures is one thing. Going round telling people what you saw between consciousness and unconsciousness is another.

That comes into the same category as describing your dreams; if you don't watch it, it can become damned boring."

For the second time that morning, anger welled up in her, and this time she did not try to check it.

"The man and the goat—"

"For Pete's sake don't start it all again," he begged. He took her chin in his hand and bent and rubbed his nose gently against hers. "I'm tired of them both. I'm going sailing; are you coming?"

"No."

"Have it your own way. What time do you want me to show up for dinner?"

"About eight, if you can."

He did not come, and Jody was not surprised. They had agreed early in their association that given perfect conditions at sea, nobody could be expected to leave them and attend purposeless functions on land. She hoped he would come, for they had parted coolly—but she was not unduly depressed when he failed to appear. Men were men, and they seemed on the whole unreasonable creatures. The reflection gave her a moment's uneasiness; perhaps she had inherited some of her aunt's intense dislike of the sex.

In spite of the absence of Charles—perhaps even because of it—dinner was very gay. Michael and Estelle had driven almost all day, and had had lunch and tea with friends. Best of all, Michael had bought Fenella a very small tent, and this was now erected in the gallery, and in it—or half in it—was Fenella's mattress, and on the mattress lay Fenella, not yet asleep, but blissfully happy in the thought of being in a camp of her own.

She was still awake when Jody went upstairs after washing up the dinner things. There was no sound in the tent, but two small, bare feet were sticking out of the opening, and the toes were wriggling.

"Hey there," called Jody softly.

Fenella's head appeared, her soft straight hair standing on end.

"I'm sleeping in a camp," she crowed.

"That's just the point—you're not sleeping, and you should be. Shall I stay here until you settle down?"

"Can I have my breakfast in the tent tomorrow?"

"Why not? If you're camping, you're camping."

She sat cross-legged on the blanket Michael had spread outside the tent, and glanced at the letters she had picked up from the hall table and not yet had time to read.

"Read them to me," commanded Fenella.

"There's nothing to read. A bill, a receipt, and an invitation."

"To a party?"

"To a wedding."

"An' what's in the parcel?"

"A pair of earrings I sent to be mended."

"Oh. Then tell me a story. The one about the train."

"In camp," said Jody firmly, "people don't tell people stories."

This seemed sense to Fenella. She lay down again, and presently the toes ceased to wriggle and became still. Jody did not move; she would stay a moment or two more.

She stripped the wrapping from the package, little bigger than a matchbox, and wondered if the jewelers had been able to match the missing stone. She hoped so; these were her favorite earrings.

She took out the inner package and gently unrolled the tissue paper. But it was not a pair of earrings that dropped into her palm. For some moments she sat motionless, looking at the tiny object she was holding.

Not more than an inch in height, beautifully carved and colored, it was a miniature of the goat named Betsy.

# CHAPTER
# 7

LADY CLEEVE FOUND that to scheme was one thing; to become entangled in the schemes was quite another. So a week later, driven by circumstances beyond her control, she paid a visit to Broome.

She came unheralded, arriving in a hired Rolls Royce; she seldom left London, but when she did, she left in comfort, not to say style.

The car drew up before the house and the chauffeur assisted her to alight. She rang the bell preemptorily, once and then again, but nobody answered her summons. The hall door stood open, but all was silence within.

Then Fenella appeared on the staircase, and after peering through the banisters at the visitor, came down to make a closer inspection.

"In case you've forgotten me, I'm your great-aunt Essie," said Lady Cleeve. "Is your mother in?"

Fenella shook her head vigorously.

"Mummy's out. Daddy's out too. Aunt Jody's out too."

"I see. When do you expect them back?"

"Mm?"

"Will they be long?"

Fenella considered.

"Mummy's picking fruit to put in bottles, and Daddy's washing the car and Aunt Jody's gone to the shops in the village."

"Then I'll wait for her." Lady Cleeve walked into the drawing room, settled herself on a sofa and sat looking round at the piles of sheet music, the music stands, the open, glossy grand piano.

"Shall I call Mummy?" inquired Fenella. She had seated herself on the piano stool and with one hand was following the smooth white notes. Like the visitor, she did not exert herself to please; like Lady Cleeve, she was calm, natural and completely at ease.

"No, don't call her. I've come to see your Aunt Jody."

"Oh. When I grow up," volunteered Fenella, "I'm going to be a man."

"Not a felicitious choice, in my opinion," commented her great-aunt.

"An' I'm going to live in a tent."

"Then take my advice and live in a warm climate."

"An' I'm going to sleep in a bag."

"You've made some finger marks on the piano keys; I should clean them if I were you."

Fenella examined the marks, licked a corner of her dress and wiped the keys clean. Lady Cleeve, nauseated, closed her eyes.

"Shall I play the piano?" offered Fenella.

"Thank you, no. Would you fetch me a book to read while I'm waiting, please?"

Fenella slid off the piano stool, chose the largest volume from a book shelf and staggered with it to the visitor.

"*Court Music of the Nineteenth Century*. Thank you," said Lady Cleeve drily. "I can't think of anything I'd like to read more." She placed the book on the sofa beside her. "Will you please go and ask the chauffeur to drive the car round to the side of the house."

"Ask who?"

"The man who is sitting in the car. The driver."

Fenella departed, chanting as she went varied versions of the message. Lady Cleeve, glancing through the long window, saw coming across the fields a figure she recognized as Jody's.

Jody, coming into the room a few minutes later, greeted her aunt with undisguised astonishment.

"This is a great surprise—but a nice one," she said, kissing her. "Have you come to lunch?"

"No. I'm on my way home; I spent the night with poor old Mildred Eaton at Eastbourne."

"Uncle Bruce's cousin?"

"Yes. He made me promise I'd look her up. She's over eighty and she's summoning all her friends and relations and making elaborate farewells, but she'll last for another ten years yet. But that wasn't what I came to talk about." She folded her hands on her lap and regarded her niece steadily. "Jody, you've got to do something about this young man."

"This . . . young man?"

"This naval man you produced from nowhere. I can't, I really cannot stand any more of him."

"You've . . . you've seen him again?" asked Jody.

"Seen him?" Lady Cleeve sounded outraged. "My dear girl, the man has all but taken up residence. He calls daily. He calls on the flimsiest excuses, he sits in my drawing room and completely ignores polite hints or broad hints. He's impervious to snubs. He has mesmerized Clarice, and she lets him in in spite of my orders to her to tell him that I'm not at home. He arrives with enormous bunches of flowers, and the place is beginning to look like a conservatory. I sit waiting for him to go away, and he pretends not to notice; he merely goes on talking as though I were entranced by his company. You must, you really must put a stop to it."

"But . . ."

"The only reason for it, of course, is that he's hoping to meet you again. He thinks that one evening, you'll drop in on your way home from work. He won't come down here, because most unfortunately I told him on the first evening that I had advised you to say nothing of your having met him." She paused. "Did you say anything?"

"No."

A long silence ensued. Jody, staring at the piano, carefully counted from middle C to the B above it . . . seven notes. Seven goats. Seven tiny representations of Betsy, all in wood, all gaily painted. Seven. One a day, beginning last Saturday. No word; simply a goat.

She wondered whether she should tell her aunt about them, and decided against it. Desmond Huntley was in trouble enough.

"I wish to heaven," said Lady Cleeve, "that I'd never overheard that conversation in the coach."

"I'm glad you did. It made me happy to—"

"—to know that the man and the goat really existed? Why couldn't it have stopped there? Why should I have been saddled with this . . . this incubus? Why should every chair in my drawing room be ruined by having this oversized interloper sitting on them every evening? If he wants to see you and can't come down here, why doesn't he take up his position outside your office? Jody, I've had as much as I can stand."

"What can I do?"

"You can come up tomorrow, confront him when he appears and tell him with my compliments to go away and stay away."

"But—"

"Here's Estelle. I can't discuss it any more. See me to my car when I leave."

Estelle came in a moment later, slim and cool in a wide-skirted cotton dress. She kissed her aunt and sat beside her on the sofa.

"I'm so sorry Michael couldn't come in with me," she began. "He—"

"You needn't make any apologies for him," Lady Cleeve spoke drily. "I had the car put where he could see it in time to invent an excuse for not coming in."

Estelle laughed.

"He didn't have to invent an excuse," she said. "He had an appointment with a parent."

"A titled one, of course?"

"Aunt Essie!" protested Jody. "You're being a bit harsh, aren't you?"

"I'm getting a little of my own back," said Lady Cleeve. "Do you know how many letters and telephone calls I answer from prospective parents to whom he has given my name—without any reference to me?"

"Can he help it if you're a Countess?" asked Estelle.

"He certainly doesn't mind using people when it suits him," said Lady Cleeve. "He—"

"He's coming," said Estelle, her eyes on the window. "And he's bringing the parent with him."

"I might have known." Lady Cleeve sounded resigned. "I'm glad you're both so amused."

Jody heard footsteps in the hall, and tried to compose her countenance, but she was still smiling when her brother-in-law opened the door.

And then the smile froze on her lips, for the woman he was ushering in was Lady Wigram.

"Estelle"—Michael spoke in the voice he reserved for parents: slow, calm, casual—"this is Lady Wigram. She wanted to meet you."

"Do come and sit down. This chair, I think; it's nice and

comfortable," said Estelle. "This is my aunt, Lady Cleeve, and this is—"

"Oh!" Lady Wigram, having bowed to Jody's aunt, was now standing before Jody, looking delighted. "We've met before. How nice to see you again!"

"You've met before?" asked Michael.

"Miss Hern came into my garden to see my goat," Lady Wigram told him. "Wasn't it odd that she should have seen it without knowing where it was?"

"Very odd indeed," said Michael.

"And wasn't it extraordinary that my brother should have found her at Lady Cleeve's house?"

"Extraordinary," said Michael. "May I offer you a drink?"

Lady Wigram could not, she said, stop for more than a moment. She had merely wanted to see the school, meet the Headmaster—

"Were you recommended to the school?" asked Michael.

"Well"—she turned her pretty, plump face to him—"I'd always heard about it, but it was my brother who sent me."

"I see," said Michael.

"He was horrified when he found that I hadn't put my sons' names down for a prep school, and I promised him I'd ring up and make an appointment at once."

"Quite so," said Michael.

"My husband and I own a cottage down here in Sussex— about six miles away," went on Lady Wigram. "We don't often use it, because we have so much to do in London, but my brother is home on leave—he's in the Navy. I suppose your sister-in-law told you?"

"No, No, she didn't mention it," said Michael.

"He's persuaded me to come and spend the rest of the summer at the cottage. He's got a boat, and he's going to do a lot of sailing." She turned to Estelle. "When we're settled, I do hope you'll all come to see us. And then we can arrange all the details about when the boys are to come."

Estelle was understood to say that she would be charmed. Lady Cleeve and Jody said nothing. Michael bowed. And then the visitor had made her farewells and was being escorted by her host and hostess to the car she had left outside the school buildings.

"What did I tell you?" said Lady Cleeve, when the door had closed behind them.

Jody turned and looked at her.

"It's . . . it's just coincidence," she said.

"Really?" Lady Cleeve rose. "I hope you'll be able to convince Michael of that. Did you see his face?"

"I . . . yes."

"If I were you, I'd put up the storm shutters."

"Why can't you stay to lunch and—"

"No. Clarice is away visiting some of her relations for three days, and I want to get home and enjoy being alone. And something tells me," she said, going to the door, "that my evenings in future will be undisturbed. This Lieutenant-Commander is a resourceful young man. Incidentally, how is Charles?"

"He's very well, thank you."

"Sailing, naturally?"

"Yes. He's . . . he went across to Saint-Malo; he's trying out a new boat. He should be back soon."

They walked in silence to the front door; the car circled to meet them; the chauffeur sprang down, removed his cap reverently and assisted his passenger in. Lady Cleeve settled herself against the cushions and then leaned out to say a last word to Jody.

"I don't think the young man will be troubling me again. I pass him over to Estelle, with my love. Don't let Michael bully you. Goodbye."

She was borne away. Jody, making a detour to avoid meeting Estelle and Michael, ran straight into them round the corner of the house, and complied meekly with her brother-in-law's request to accompany them to the house.

"Don't you," he asked when they were once more indoors, "owe us some sort of explanation?"

"Of course she doesn't," said Estelle. "Don't be so pompous." She turned to her sister. "But Jody, you pig, fancy not telling me."

"Well, you all felt that it was stupid to go on talking about the accident, and—"

"Would you please tell us what happened?" said Michael.

Haltingly, stumblingly, Jody told the story. She spoke of her aunt's information and her subsequent visit to Waverley Square. She told them of her entry into the garden, and Desmond Huntley's visit to her aunt's house that evening.

Of her subsequent visit to Dorset Court with Desmond Huntley she said nothing. She had time in which to ponder the matter, and she had seven goats to help her to a conclusion. The visit had been a mistake. Mr. Kennedy had been melodramatic, and she had been foolish to allow herself to set out on a road that could lead nowhere. She regretted having gone so far; for all Desmond Huntley's professed disinterestedness, it was clear that he was using methods all his own to advance their acquaintanceship.

The yellow brick road led nowhere—and even if it did, she would not be on it with Desmond Huntley.

"You mean to tell me," asked Michael slowly, "that this fellow turned up and told you—"

"—that he was the man with the goat? I knew it before he said anything. I recognized him."

"And I suppose he told you not to say anything to us?"

"No. Aunt Essie said it would be silly to talk to you about it."

"My God!" Michael turned in wonder to his wife. "She falls down some stairs, she's told it would be safer to forget the whole thing—and what does she do? She goes roaming around London listening for goats. She walks into a total stranger's garden, and then she gets involved with a naval fellow with too much time on his hands. And now—"

"Now you've got two new pupils," Estelle reminded him. "What are you complaining about?"

"How much of this did you tell Charles?" Michael asked Jody.

"I didn't tell him anything."

"Well, don't." Michael spoke in his most abrupt manner. "If you want to preserve the peace, then for the Lord's sake, keep quiet. If Charles gets to know that a stray Lieutenant-Commander has come wandering into your life, bringing a goat with him—"

"I would have told him if he hadn't said that the subject bored him."

"He wouldn't have found it as boring as he thought," said Michael shrewdly. "But since he knows nothing about it, let him go on knowing nothing about it. I'll keep an eye on this Huntley fellow, and if he shows any signs of getting above himself, I'll deal with him. If Charles thinks he's down here to make trouble, then there'll be trouble—and it won't be Huntley who makes it."

"If he's coming to live in the cottage with his sister," pointed out Estelle, "they're bound to come here, and Charles will have to know who he is."

"Why will he, unless Jody shows an interest in him? Look," said Michael reasonably, "I don't know exactly how Lady Wigram came to decide that she'd send her two sons here. All I know is that Wigram's a baronet, a Member of Parliament, and a man of wealth and influence. If his wife was influenced by her brother, and if her brother is fixing the school angle and the country-cottage angle with a view to seeing Jody at closer quarters, we don't have to worry about it yet—or worry Charles about it yet. I want the two boys, and I won't get them if we start a movement to keep Lady Wigram's brother off the premises. Jody's old enough to deal with anybody who tries to jump fences. If she wants any help, she can come to me—but if we make a start by getting Charles's back up, I can say goodbye to the Wigrams. Does that make sense?"

"It might make sense, but it also makes things a bit difficult for Jody, doesn't it?" asked Estelle. "She's engaged to Charles."

"Does that mean that she has to hand him a list of all the men who make passes at her?"

"No, but—"

Michael turned to Jody.

"All right. Tell him what you like," he said, "But don't tell him just yet."

"I can't tell him just yet," said Jody. "He's at Saint-Malo."

Michael stared at her in surprise.

"For the day?"

"For four days. He went yesterday."

"In *Gazelle*, or crewing for somebody else?"

"In *Ballerina*. He's thinking of buying her from the Major."

Michael began to speak, thought better of it, and walked out of the room. Estelle's eyes rested thoughtfully on her sister.

"Did you and Charles have a row?"

"No."

"You've been odd lately. Is everything all right between you?"

Jody did not answer for a time. She was standing by the piano, absently picking out an air with one finger. Her expression was a sober, almost brooding.

"What is it, Jody?" asked Estelle gently at last.

Jody looked up.

"Nothing much," she said. "Just a sort of silly idea I've got that Charles and Michael push me around."

"Charles and Michael push everyone around."

"I know. I suppose you and I ought to be used to it. But I must be getting more . . . more demanding or something."

"Your accident shook you up."

"Perhaps. But I would have thought that when something like that happened to anybody, there'd be no harm in treating it as a major event. Falling downstairs is nothing, and nobody wants to make a fuss about it, but there were circumstances—"

"The doctor told us quite firmly that we weren't to let you dwell on it."

"And Charles told me quite firmly that if I went on dwelling on it, I'd become a bore. That's to say, even if I found talking a relief, he'd rather not talk. And Michael doesn't really mind how much trouble Lady Wigram's brother can cause, just as long as the waiting list grows longer."

"I know it sounded like that, but what Michael was really saying was that the whole business of the brother was quite unimportant to him and to you and to Charles—provided that you yourself had no interest in him." She paused. "Have you?"

"No. Yes," amended Jody. "He was kind, and I liked him. He took me to Dorset Court and tried to clear up a few things."

"You didn't mention that before."

"I know. And I'd rather you didn't mention it to Michael —but I did feel for a time that I'd like to go on finding out things—if there were any things to find out."

"What made you change your mind?"

"Realizing how easy it is to start something, and how difficult it is to stop it."

"Meaning this Desmond Huntley?"

"Yes."

"Michael wasn't pushing you around just now. He was just suggesting that we needn't meet trouble halfway, that's all. So what's really worrying you is that Charles has gone off to Saint-Malo."

"He's been before, and he'll go again, and I like him to go. I like him to do what he likes doing, but . . ."

"But?"

"He hasn't once asked me what I'd like to do. And Michael stood here just now and calmly mapped out what we were all going to do, without once asking me what I thought of Desmond Huntley. There's no danger of my thinking at all about him—but it's nice to be asked."

"If you marry Charles, you won't be asked. He's like Michael. I've often wondered why the two of them have been friends for so long, because they're both selfish, they're both pigheaded, and they're both entirely unconcerned with other people's reactions or feelings or preferences. But aren't most men like that?"

"How would we know? Michael and Charles were about the first men we had anything to do with, and they proposed and we accepted them. That doesn't teach us much about men, does it?"

Estelle sat on the arm of a chair and spoke thoughtfully.

"It works out," she said. "If you've got any intelligence and if you're not too starry-eyed about a man, you can sum him up pretty well before you marry him. You take him as he is. Sometimes you'd rather have him changed in this way or in that, but on the whole you're happy putting up with him as he is. If that isn't romance, it's something better: it's marriage. You've known Charles since you were fourteen; you ought to have come to a lot of unsatisfying conclusions about him before now—but you love him and you agreed to marry him and now's the time to clear up any doubts you may have."

"I haven't any doubts. It's just—"

"Michael always said that as a family, we've more head than heart—and it may be true," said Estelle. "Look at Aunt Essie. Look at me. I love Michael and I can't imagine life without him, but I've never experienced any of those embrace-me-or-I-die moments you read about in books. I can never understand how these women find time for the ordinary, routine business of living. There they always are, and there the divan always is, ready for the next burning scene. I don't know how they find men with the necessary time, either. Certainly the Michaels and the Charleses of the world have most of their mind on other things."

Jody said nothing. Sitting on alone when Estelle had gone in search of Fenella, she found nothing in the conversation to soothe her unusually ruffled feelings.

Her thoughts went to Desmond Huntley. However much

he had done to influence his sister, it was certain that he had not taken her into his confidence, for her surprise at seeing Jody had been obviously genuine. But one fact stood out clearly: that he would soon have an excuse, if he needed one, for becoming acquainted with Estelle and her husband. He would be living nearby, and he would be a visitor; perhaps a frequent one, for Lady Cleeve had testified to his staying powers.

Deep down, she felt the stirrings of fear. Desmond Huntley was approaching in ever-narrowing circles, and with him came the memory of things she would rather forget.

Desmond Huntley's interest lay, she felt sure, only partly in herself; she was the passport without which he could not travel further along a road which promised adventure. He was home on leave, he had time to spare, and he had touched the fringes of a mystery; she could not blame him for wanting to probe further.

She was recalled to the present by Fenella, who came in to demand food.

"My lunch," she explained. "Not my lunch to eat at table, but to eat—"

"In camp?"

"Yes. Why can't I have sausages fried like the boys? I'm tired of having sandwiches and eating them on the floor. Why can't I cook things in a tin like the boys? Why can't I have a kettle on a hook, with—"

"Whoa!" said Jody. "Why can't you eat a nice picnic lunch in the sunshine, instead of crouching in that tent in the gallery?"

"Cos' I'm camping. I want to take the tent outside and live inside it, but Mummy won't let me. Why won't she let me? Why can't I—"

"Cold leg of chicken, beans in a bowl with tomato sauce, lettuce and tomato and beetroot and watercress and apple and carrots all chopped up nicely into a salad in another bowl, and a choc-ice. Take it or leave it."

Fenella took it. Jody, with a view to avoiding any more awkward discussions with her brother-in-law, elected to share the camp meal, and ate it seated cross-legged with Fenella outside the tent. It was uncomfortable, but it was better than being cross-examined.

She was carrying the empty plates and bowls down the

stairs when the telephone rang, and she put the loaded tray on the hall table and picked up the receiver. To her astonishment, her aunt's voice came to her ears.

"Jody?"

"Yes, Aunt Essie."

"I've just got home. Can you come?"

There was something strained in her aunt's voice, and Jody's heart began to beat fast.

"Are you all right, Aunt Essie?"

"I'm perfectly all right. Tell Estelle I'm finding it difficult to manage without Clarice, and come as soon as you can."

"Has something happened?"

"Yes," said Lady Cleeve.

"What—?"

There was no point in finishing the question. Lady Cleeve had rung off.

## CHAPTER
# 8

AN HOUR AND A HALF later, Jody stood in the drawing room
of the house at Knightsbridge and looked slowly round her.

Beside her, Lady Cleeve waited in silence.

The scene was one of devastation. Chairs and sofas had
been pushed aside, drawers pulled out and their contents
scattered. Ornaments lay on the carpet, books lay in heaps.

Jody turned slowly to look at her aunt.

"The other rooms—?"

"Just the same. Except the kitchen and the bathroom.
They were kind enough to spare those."

Jody drew a long breath.

"What's missing, Aunt Essie?"

"Nothing whatsoever," said Lady Cleeve.

Jody, silent from sheer astonishment, could only stare. Her
aunt smiled grimly.

"Like you, I couldn't believe it at first," she said. "But it's
true. Nothing has been taken. But every drawer in every
room has been ransacked."

"Have you phoned the police?"

"No."

"But . . . but why not?"

"Because I wanted to talk to you first."

"How did they get in?"

"They used a key. None of the locks was touched, none of
the windows opened. Whoever it was came in, looked for
what they wanted, found it and went away."

"But you said—"

"Sit down," said Lady Cleeve, "and I'll explain."

Jody sat down.

"I said that nothing was missing," began Lady Cleeve,
"but I was answering the question you meant to put: what
had they taken in money or effects. Nothing of that sort was
touched. But somebody has been through all the papers I

keep in the house. Every place in which documents could have been kept was turned inside out. The safe was broken into, but nothing of value was taken—but again, the papers had been looked through."

"But . . . but why?"

"I don't know."

"What did they take away?"

"Everything," answered Lady Cleeve, "that related to you."

There was silence. Jody, in a fog of bewilderment, waited for her aunt to speak again, and presently Lady Cleeve walked across the room and lifted a sheaf of papers from the littered desk.

"You see these?" she asked. "They all relate to you and Estelle. Copies of your father's will and your mother's will. School bills. Bills incurred by you both after you'd left school. In the safe were details of the stocks you and Estelle hold. Everything connected with Estelle is still where it was. Everything to do with you has vanished."

"But"—Jody frowned—"are you absolutely certain that—"

"—that all the missing papers related to you? Perfectly certain. I didn't realize it at first, of course; when I saw that the silver and ornaments were intact, I thought they had been looking for money. I didn't have much in the house, but what there was, was untouched. No jewels were missing, as I told you. If I'd been a woman with a shady past, I would have thought that somebody was looking for an incriminating letter of some kind; having no complications of that kind to worry me, I began to wonder exactly which papers had gone. And you can see for yourself; everything with your name on it. Vanished."

Jody turned to study the older woman.

"You came home and found everything like this?"

"Yes."

"But . . . but weren't you frightened? You were alone, and they might have been hiding somewhere."

"In which case, I wouldn't have been alone," pointed out Lady Cleeve.

"But you should have called somebody, rung up—"

"When I closed the front door and came in here and saw what you're seeing now," said her aunt slowly, "I just stood in the middle of it all, trembling. I was shaking from head to foot—and then I realized that I wasn't trembling with fear. It was anger." Her voice deepened. "I was so angry that I could scarcely breathe. Someone had dared to come in while I was out; someone had dared to put their hands on my things, my lovely things. If I'd imagined such a thing happening, I would have been frightened—but walking in and seeing it was different." She took a deep breath. "I used to think that people who heard thieves in the night and seized a poker and went looking for them were rather brave—but now I know that they were simply acting from instinct. I wasn't frightened. I was just sick with anger. I walked into every room, searching, hoping to find whoever it was who had done it. I didn't even have the poker. I had my bare hands, and a horrible, primitive desire to use them."

"How long do you think they were here?"

"I don't know. I left the house at six o'clock yesterday evening. Clarice had already gone. I got back about half an hour before I rang you up."

"Aren't you going to ring up the police now?"

Lady Cleeve hesitated.

"I'd like to. But if I do—"

"If you do," said Jody slowly, "I suppose they'll jump to the conclusion that this is something out of *my* shady past?"

"Something of that sort. How could I convince them that nothing of this kind has ever happened to us before? How could I tell a skeptical police officer that you've never in all your life had any connection with anybody who could possibly want to hurt you or to injure you? Once I've called in the police, they'll begin questioning you. From here, they'll go down to Broome and then we shall have real trouble. If ever anything happened—"

"You needn't go on," said Jody. "I know. If any scandal threatened the school, Michael would never forgive me. Nor would Estelle."

"And that's why I didn't call the police. Once they began to probe, who knows where they'd stop? Before we knew where we were, they would have been harking back to your accident and trying to prove that this was in some way connected with it."

"Well, isn't it?" asked Jody.

Lady Cleeve stared at her.

"What do you mean?"

Jody's miserable gaze was on a sofa cushion; her finger plucked absently at its fringe.

"I don't know. I don't know, Aunt Essie," she said. "But what else could it be? There's no mystery about any of us—or there wasn't until I fell down those stairs at Dorset Court."

"But if this is connected with the accident, and if you did get involved in some way we don't understand with shady people, why should they come to this house to look for papers connected with you? Why wouldn't they go down to Broome, where you live?"

Jody raised frightened eyes to her aunt's.

"Perhaps they will," she said.

Lady Cleeve walked to the window and stood staring out, and something in her attitude made Jody rise and go to stand beside her.

"There's nothing to worry about, Aunt Essie."

"No?" Lady Cleeve turned to face her. "You're the only person in the world I really care deeply about, and you're mixed up with who knows what, and you tell me there's nothing to worry about!" Her gaze went round the room. "They had a whole night and a whole morning to find what they were looking for. They had time to look slowly and systematically. So why all this mess—have you stopped to think why?"

"Because they didn't come last night; they must have come this morning and done the job in a hurry."

"Perhaps. But I don't think they were in a hurry. I think . . . I think they left the place like this on purpose."

"You mean . . . to advertise their visit?"

"Yes."

"Why would they do that?" asked Jody slowly.

"To frighten somebody. And as I don't think they have any interest in me, they can only have done it to frighten you."

"Because I . . . because I went back to Dorset Court and found out that I'd called at the wrong flat?"

"What else?" Lady Cleeve's long, white hands fluttered for a moment. "What else? And . . . it was I who urged you to go. I . . . I encouraged you to go."

"And I'm glad I went," said Jody quietly. "I'm sorry about what's happened to the house—but I'm glad I found out just a little of what happened that morning."

"Are you going to tell Commander Huntley about it?"

Jody hesitated.

"I . . . I don't know. I don't think so. Because whatever the mystery about that morning is—if there is a mystery—one thing's only too clear, and that is that everything that happens to me affects you and Estelle and Michael and Charles. Your house has been turned upside down, and we're afraid to go to the police—why? In case we involve Estelle and Michael."

Lady Cleeve said nothing. In silence, they began to set the house to rights again; in silence they made tea; they drank it saying little, each absorbed in thought.

But when Jody announced her intention of staying the night, her aunt would not hear of it.

"No. I've been thinking it over," she said. "It's quite obvious that nobody's anxious to come face to face with me; that's why they chose a time when I was out of the house. And they're not interested in anything of mine. Go home and say nothing, and let me know at once if trouble follows you down to Estelle's."

"But I can't let you sleep in the house alone!"

"Why not? I shall keep a poker beside me."

"Two pokers are better than one."

"You're going home," said Lady Cleeve firmly, "and you're going to put this out of your mind, if you can, and go on with your life as though nothing had happened. I wish I could put forward one single, sensible theory as to who entered the house, and why—but my mind is a blank. The whole thing is too complicated. All we can do is conjecture, and fabricate wild possibilities, and go round in circles and end up just where we are now—in the dark. Go home—and don't tell them what has happened."

Jody went home. When she got there, she found cars assembled in the drive, and brought her mind with difficulty to the present. Cars: concert: audience. Memory returning, she felt sorry for the audience, for tonight the Professor's longest and, in Jody's opinion, most dreary work was to be performed: "Variations on a Theme by Bach." It went on for so long that it would occupy the entire first half of the program.

She went upstairs and changed, and then went into the kitchen to make her usual preparations for coffee. Miss Bishop in the drawing room, made a swift count and took the result to Jody.

"Thirty-five," she told her. "Quite a good number, don't

you think?" she handed Jody a cashbox. "That's the collection I took at the door for charity. It feels heavy, doesn't it? The chairs are nearly all full."

"What do I do with latecomers?"

"Oh, I don't think any more people will come," said Miss Bishop, on her way out. "We're rather late as it is. Finding seats for any more will be rather difficult. I'm sure you can close the front door now."

Jody, going out a few moments later to close it, found herself brought up abruptly by a massive form, and looked up.

"Oh," she said.

Desmond Huntley smiled at her, and proffered a small green ticket.

"My sister couldn't come, and sends her apologies," he said. "I've come instead."

"Ah," said Jody.

"You're very talkative tonight."

"I was wondering where I could find you a seat," she said coldly.

She was glad to see him lose a little of his confidence. Through the open door of the drawing room could be seen the audience, sober and intent. The Trio, bows poised, awaited the Professor's signal, and then the music began.

"If you'll very kindly give me your contribution to the charity—" began Jody in an undertone.

He plunged a hand into a pocket, brought out a note, and handed it to her.

"All seats full," he said, satisfaction in his voice.

"I can find room for you," said Jody. "There's a chair there, between Mrs. Birks and General Beddington."

"But look here—"

"This way," said Jody.

He followed her, whispering hoarse appeals as he came.

"Look, don't be harsh. I only came to . . . I mean, I'm not . . . you see, this isn't quite my kind of music, and—"

Bending, whispering, apologizing, she waved him along the row to the vacant seat, and stood watching his stumbling progress. He knocked the Vicar's wife's handbag off her lap, plunged to retrieve it and caused a minor earthquake in the row in front. Proceeding, he stood upon the Vicar's foot, mumbled an apology, brought an angry series of Shhs! from the disturbed listeners, and fell awkwardly into the seat allotted to him.

Satisfied, Jody went back to the kitchen and prepared coffee. That would teach people to flood the mailbags with goats.

He came to her, pale and wild-eyed, in the interval. She was behind a large table in the hall, serving coffee and biscuits, and he pushed his way slowly to her side.

"Coffee?" she asked him.

"Strong and black, please."

She handed it to him.

"The second half of the program," she told him, "is going to be interesting. The Professor—"

He looked round and spoke cautiously.

"How much does one have to pay to get out?"

"You're not musical?"

"That's just it; I am. Do you have much of this kind of thing?"

"Haven't you heard of Professor Joachim's String Trio?"

"Is that who they were? Is the Professor the cellist? Yes, of course he is," he answered himself. "And the violinist is the fellow who owns *Ballerina*. Versatile, isn't he?" He paused. "You know something? I've arranged to have a berth of my own at that toy harbor—what's it called? Marcove. I spoke to the chaps up at the Tar Barrel, and they told me to wait until Charles Vaughan—your fiancé—could see me about it. But he was over at Saint-Malo—why aren't you with him? —and I got hold of the Major and he says he'll try to fix me up. Order of line in the future: *Ballerina*, *Gazelle*, *Wavecrest*, the last skippered by myself. She's a lovely little thing; you'll like her. Is that your brother-in-law talking to the Duke?"

"Yes."

"And your sister's over there?"

"Yes."

"I'd very much like to meet them."

But Michael, who missed nothing, had attached the Duke to a nearby group, disengaged himself gracefully, and was walking into the hall and toward the coffee table.

"I think," he said at once to Desmond, "you must be Lady Wigram's brother."

"Yes. How d'you do?"

"You must meet my wife; she's just coming. Estelle," he went on, as she came up, "this is the fellow who was responsible for Jody's goat complex. Commander Huntley—my wife."

They bowed, quite clearly delighted with one another.

"You gave us a lot of trouble," said Estelle. "We thought you were hallucinations."

"The stuff of dreams." Michael's glance flickered calculatingly over Desmond's bulky form. "Several hundred pounds worth of stuff. Pity Charles isn't here; he would have like to meet you. Charles," he added easily, "is my sister-in-law's fiancé."

"I've missed him twice." Desmond's tone sounded almost genuinely regretful. "He wasn't down at Marcove this morning, when I was making arrangements to leave my boat there."

"You're . . . leaving your boat there?" inquired Michael politely.

"Yes. When I can make arrangements for her. Cheaper than Newhaven, and nearer," explained Desmond.

"Nearer to what?" Michael asked.

"To this cottage of my sister's. Only a matter of a quarter of an hour's drive."

"I see."

There was a slight pause. Michael, a very tall man, had to look up an inch or two, but the eyes of the two men met for a long and unmoving moment. Then there was a stir, and the sound of instruments being tuned, and Michael spoke.

"Back to business, I think," he said. "Estelle, will you look after the Commander?"

He walked away and detached the Duke from his group and led him back to his seat, and Desmond watched him admiringly.

"Wonderful," he murmured.

"What's wonderful?" asked Estelle.

"That shepherd's touch. Drawing the old Duke on an invisible thread—and I suppose you know that the old boy's favorite tune is the Lambeth Walk?"

Estelle laughed.

"*Noblesse oblige*," she reminded him. "It's one of the reasons I never wanted to be a Duchess. Jody, can I leave you with these things? I ought to get back to my seat."

"I'll manage," said Jody.

The hall was emptying. Jody waited for Desmond to follow the last stragglers into the drawing room, only to find that he was stacking cups and saucers.

"Which way to the kitchen?" he inquired.

"Will you please put those things down?" she requested. "You're a member of the audience and—"

"I was. I quit. Where's the kitchen?"

Argument, she saw, would be useless—and expensive; he had Estelle's best china piled in a wavering pyramid, his chin supporting the beautiful, fragile cups.

"This way," she said.

He made four journeys to and fro, and then took off his jacket and turned up his sleeves.

"Please," protested Jody, "will you—"

"Go away and leave you to wash up? No, I won't. If I wash you'll have to dry, and then I shall be able to talk to you—and I want to talk very seriously to you."

"If you're trying to make me start off on a wild goose chase looking for somebody called Laurie," said Jody, "I'm afraid you'll be wasting your time."

"I never waste time. Look at me now."

She looked at him. Elbow-deep in suds, he was handling the slippery china with surprising skill. He looked completely at home.

He fished in the soapy depths, captured a creamjug and rinsed it.

"The person I'd really like to see," he told Jody, "is your fiancé."

"I wish he were here. He'd tell you, much more forcibly than I can, that we all believe in leaving well enough alone."

"Did you tell him about Laurie?"

Jody hesitated.

"No," she said reluctantly at last.

"I needn't have asked. If you'd told him, he wouldn't be at Saint-Malo."

Jody lifted the last cup carefully from a tray and turned to face him.

"Look, Commander—"

"Good Lord!" he ejaculated in sheer astonishment. "Haven't we progressed beyond that stage? What's a Christian name between friends? It doesn't mean anything—it's just a way round awkward sentences like Commander Huntley. You were saying?"

"I was saying that there's no reason why you shouldn't go on spending your time building up a slight accident into something important, but—"

"But you've decided to call off the hounds?"

"Yes. And as we've got on to animals, would you very kindly stop sending me goats?"

"You didn't get a goat today, did you?"

"No, not today. But—"

"That's because I knew I was going to see you today. At least, I hoped I was going to see you. That meant that I could remind you myself, in person, that there were one or two things about this mystery still to be investigated, and—"

"There is no mystery," said Jody slowly and carefully. "You and I got carried away by a melodramatic gentleman calling himself Mr. Kennedy, but—"

"But even if we did, there's still a mystery," said Desmond. "And those goats serve to remind you."

"And if I don't want to be reminded?"

He said nothing for a few moments; he stood looking down at her, his expression one of mingled bewilderment and irritation.

"I don't understand you," he said slowly at last. "You or your family. I call on your aunt hoping she'll understand that I'm strong, brave and intelligent and anxious to offer myself as a deputy, an aide, a stooge—anything, just so long as I can help move this bogged-down mystery a stage further. What does she do? She freezes me out. Why did I go to her instead of coming here? Because I wanted her to make it clear to your other relations, and your future relations, that I wasn't bull-dozing my way into your life with a view to annoying anybody. You're engaged; that's fine. I'm glad. I haven't met him, but he keeps a nice line in boats. I hope you'll be very happy. But in the meantime, what's got into everybody?"

"Everybody is simply anxious to let well enough alone, that's all," said Jody.

"Letting well enough alone is a fine principle, and I'm all for it. But when things aren't well, when there are circumstances about that accident of yours that cry to Heaven to be investigated—"

"—then we'll still leave well alone," she ended.

"I see." He took a pile of crockery from the table and placed it on the sink. "You're all going to cut the incident out of your lives, put in a patch and proceed as though nothing had happened?"

"Yes. Doctor's orders. He said, and Michael and Charles agreed with him, that it wasn't healthy to dwell on things like this."

"But haven't you told them that we found a lead, that we had a good chance of finding out—"

"No. All I told my sister and my brother-in-law was that I'd traced you and the goat. I wouldn't have told them that if your sister hadn't greeted me like an old friend when she came here. If I told them that you and I had gone to Dorset Court and . . . Just imagine how it sounds in cold blood: the man with the goat turned up and we found that the people whose flat I went to by mistake fled to Kenya, and one of them was a blonde and there was blood on the carpet. If one of your friends or relations came to you with a story like that, would you take it seriously?"

"It would depend who told the story. If a sane, cool-headed girl like you said anything, I've give it my attention." He placed the last piece of china on the draining-board and dried his hands thoughtfully. "But as far as you and your sister and brother-in-law and fiancé are concerned—we leave it just where it is?"

"Yes."

"Funny, isn't it?" he mused. "The watchword of half the English nation is: don't get mixed up in it. I can hear my late mother saying it: 'Never get yourself needlessly involved, my dear boy. Never risk getting mixed up with anything shady. Give people of That Sort a wide berth.'"

"Isn't that the soundest of sound advice?"

"Normally speaking, yes. But this is different. How can you all pretend that what happened to you that morning was simply an accident? Your relations might still be in the dark about recent developments, but you can't have any lingering illusions. Take the facts: you're sensible, extremely self-possessed, not previously given to fainting, and if my guess is right, plucky. You're found at the foot of a stone staircase, unconscious. Did you fall down the stairs? If you did, were you bruised? Skin scraped? Arms or legs injured? No."

"You've been talking to the Major."

"Wrong. The Major has been talking to me. And what he pointed out was something I should have figured out for myself. And would have figured out for myself if Kennedy hadn't given us something else to think about. You got a knock right on the top of your head. To get an injury in that place when falling downstairs, you'd have had to take a dive —and if you'd taken a dive, you wouldn't be here now, discussing it. Whether you went to the Grierson's apartment or not, we don't know—but why did they leave just afterwards in a hurry? Was that just coincidence?"

"Does it matter much?" asked Jody.

Something in her voice checked him as he was about to answer. He took her arm and turned her slowly to the light.

"Something's happened since I last saw you," he said slowly. "You're keeping something back. What is it?"

"Somebody broke into my aunt's flat and ransacked it."

He stared at her.

"Thieves?"

"No. The maid was away, and my aunt spent the night with a friend. When she got home, she found that someone had entered the house—with a key; they didn't break in. And they didn't steal anything except papers."

"Papers?"

"Every paper concerning me. That's all."

"When did this happen?"

"Last night or this morning."

"And"—his voice was incredulous—"you've said nothing about it to your brother-in-law?"

"No. Can't you see why? No, perhaps you can't; you didn't see my aunt's house looking as I saw it today. Everything thrown about, all her lovely things . . ." Her voice trembled, and she paused to steady it. "That's what happened to her, and that's what might happen to Estelle. And I think it happened because you and I went to Dorset Court and asked questions. And I'm frightened. I don't think I'm frightened for myself, because I learned with you the other day, and with my aunt today, that curiosity can be stronger than fear—but I'm frightened of involving other people, people I love. You don't know what this school means to Michael. He bought it ten years ago as a dying concern, and he's built it up all by himself, and you can see what would happen if the police came round. How could Charles go on getting jobs as a tutor if people got to know we were mixed up with the police?"

" 'Mixed up with the police' . . . You make them sound

like undesirables who've got to be kept away at all costs—
Jody don't you want to know what really happened?"

"I . . . yes." Her answer came unwillingly at last. "For
myself—entirely for myself, I'd like to know exactly what I
did that morning. But there's no way of finding out without
dragging other people in, and so I'm going to leave things as
they are."

He said no more. Presently he went away and she went
slowly upstairs to her room. The sound of the music pursued
her, and she wondered whether Fenella—still camping in her
tent in the gallery—had been disturbed. But the two little
feet sticking out of the tent were still relaxed, and a cautious
look showed Fenella fast asleep on her mattress, her arms
out-flung and almost touching the sides of the tent.

Jody slept badly. Going down to prepare breakfast, she
found that neither Estelle nor Michael were downstairs; yells
from their bedroom indicated that Fenella was playing an
early-morning game with her parents.

The drawing room was in disorder, and Jody tidied it; the
task took longer than she anticipated, and she had to snatch
a hasty breakfast and hurry away to the bus stop. She
paused in the hall to extract the letters from the box, take
her own mail and drop the rest on the hall table. Then she
was hurrying along the lane that led to the crossroads.

The two letters, thrust hastily into her handbag, remained
there, forgotten, until she had got off the bus and was waiting for the train. She took them out and glanced at them;
one was a receipt, the other a plain envelope with a typed
address and a London postmark.

She opened it in the train. The message was brief, and—
like the address—typewritten. It read:

COME ALONE. MERLIN BAR. MARBLE ARCH.
28TH. 7 P.M.

Today was the 28th.

## CHAPTER
# 9

FOR THE FIRST FEW moments, Jody could do no more than stare at the sheet of paper in her hand.

The Merlin Bar. The twenty-eighth. Come alone.

Slowly the noisy, crowded carriage receded and the events of the past two weeks crept into her mind and marshaled themselves for her inspection. The wrong apartment . . . an accident . . . a man calling himself Kennedy and talking of a missing couple whose name was Grierson. A house ransacked, papers stolen.

And now . . . the Merlin Bar, seven o'clock.

Sitting and gazing unseeingly out at the flying landscape, she reviewed the past few days. She had touched, with Desmond Huntley, the fringe of a mystery—and had drawn back. Now for the first time, she faced the possibility that she might not be permitted to draw back. She might wish to; others might have other views. She was in this—and somebody was seeing to it that she stayed in.

She had seen the Merlin Bar often enough, though she had only once visited it. It was almost opposite the gates of Hyde Park; a ground-floor establishment, long, brilliantly lit, fashionable, frequented for the most part by young men with loud voices and too-long hair, and girls who all seemed to look and speak alike. They ordered coffee or drinks, which were served by waiters in outfits vaguely suggesting Seville.

The bar was on a corner. Passers-by had an excellent view of the glittering interior, and it seemed to Jody the last place that would be chosen as a rendezvous by anybody desiring privacy. Nobody wishing to harm her would have chosen the Merlin Bar, resembling as it did a display tank for brightly-colored tropical fish. Nobody could meet, nothing could take place unobserved.

The Merlin Bar . . . seven P.M.

Throughout the day she worked automatically, the same

question shuttling to and fro in her mind: to go, or not to go.

And at five minutes to seven, she found herself at Marble Arch, outside the Merlin Bar.

She hesitated for one last moment before entering the bar —and then she had pushed open the large plate-glass door. She was inside.

She glanced round. Nobody seemed to be taking any interest in her arrival. All the tables were occupied, as were most of the seats at the long, curving bar. She saw a vacant stool at one end, and threaded her way toward it and perched herself on its slippery scarlet leather surface.

Looking round, she saw that she was near the door on the side opposite that at which she had entered. If she had been standing among the crowd, she would not have been able to see anyone coming or going at either entrance—but raised as she was on the high stool, she could see over the heads of those about her to the doors on either side.

She ordered sherry, and noted that she was not the only woman who had come unattended. Escorts came in, waved over intervening heads and joined the women they had come to meet; new groups entered, others broke up and dispersed —and Jody sat unregarded.

She glanced at her watch. It was two minutes to seven; the time, she told herself with a touch of grimness, was not yet. Somebody must soon approach her. Somebody . . .

And then she looked up and saw Desmond Huntley.

He had come in by the door near which she was seated. He was standing just inside the doorway, his height giving him a clear view of the company. His eyes were roving over the various groups, searching, seeking.

Jody stared at him, her mind seething with conjecture. Desmond Huntley—here. She had been told to come, and he . . .

It could not be coincidence. The Merlin Bar was not a place that would attract him. If he was here, it was because he—like herself—had been told to come.

The next moment, he had turned and seen her.

Only astonishment showed for the first few seconds on his face—and then it was followed by an emotion she could read easily enough: fear. He stared at her across the restless groups that separated them, and then he shouldered his way to her side. When at last he stood beside her, fear had gone from his face, and anger had taken its place.

"What in Heaven's name . . . what are you doing here?"

"I . . . I got a letter telling me to come. An anonymous letter. Just a typed message, telling me to come—alone."

He seemed unable, for a few seconds, to speak. Then his voice came, slow and incredulous.

"You were insane enough to . . . to . . ."

"Yes."

He seemed to consider the situation.

"You must be out of your mind," he said at last, on a hopeless note. "You must be stark, staring mad."

"Did you get a letter too?"

"Yes. But that was different. You . . ."

They stared at one another—a long, level, measuring gaze. But before Jody could voice the questions that sprang to her lips, something drew her eyes from his face. Beyond him, behind him, standing just inside one of the entrances, was a woman: young, fair, slender. Even if her beauty had not set her apart, she would have been conspicuous in that company. In that room of bleached heads and imitation furs and paste jewelry, her honey-colored hair, subdued makeup and unadorned dress drew all eyes.

Jody had little time to study her appearance, but she was completely certain that this was the woman Mr. Kennedy had described. This was Mrs. Grierson, who had occupied Apartment Number Four. This was the woman who, with her husband, had left at suspiciously short notice for an improbable-sounding address in Kenya.

She heard Desmond's voice behind her.

"My guess," he said slowly, "is that her name is Laurie."

Jody was getting down from the high stool.

"I'm going to find out," she said.

"If you ask her, how do you know she'll tell you?" Desmond asked.

Jody made no reply. She had no clear idea of what she meant to do, but she wanted to reach the woman standing in the doorway. She took a step forward, and found Desmond's hand gripping her arm and holding her prisoner.

"Stay where you are," he said.

It was an order, whipped out with an authority that checked her. For a moment, she was still—and then she turned on him angrily.

"Let me go! I want to talk to her."

"I'll do the talking—if it *is* Laurie. You'll stay here," said Desmond grimly. "You're going to keep out of this."

"But—"

He was too late. The woman had turned. A man had opened the great plate-glass door and was ushering her outside. He led her to a large black car, handed her in, took his place beside her and drove away.

They had gone—but not before the two watching them had recognized the man who had made so brief an appearance. They had seen him before, short and fat and out of breath, standing beside Desmond's car outside Dorset Court.

Jody turned and looked at Desmond, and he spoke slowly.

"Our friend Mr. Kennedy," he said.

Anger and disappointment welled up in Jody.

"If you'd let me go to her—" she began.

He broke into her reproaches.

"We're getting out of here," he said. "Come on."

He began to lead her away, and was recalled by an outraged barman demanding payment for the sherry. Plunging a hand into his pocket, he brought out the money; then he took Jody's arm and led her to the door.

They did not speak until they had reached his car, parked on a quiet side street. He put her in, and they drove the few hundred yards that separated them from the Park, and entered its gates. Then he pulled up, switched off the engine and turned to confront her.

"Now," he said. "What do you mean by taking a crazy risk like that?"

Jody did not answer at once; she had a question of her own to put to him.

"What were you doing there?"

"Exactly what you were. Answering an anonymous summons."

For an instant, doubt leaped into her mind. No longer, in this new life, could she accept a straight answer to a straight question. She reminded herself of how little she knew about this man seated beside her. He had been anxious to form a company of two, advancing upon this unknown path they had named the yellow brick road, seeking the solution to a problem that was—she thought—hers alone. But he had appeared on the stroke of seven at the Merlin Bar—and the woman called Laurie—could that have been she . . . had entered only a few seconds after him.

To believe . . . or to disbelieve. He looked utterly straightforward. But probably so did Laurie. Laurie, who had left Dorset Court in a hurry on the morning of the accident, leaving a small bloodstain on a carpet.

She turned to find Desmond's eyes on her.

"You don't believe me," he challenged her.

"I think I do," said Jody steadily, "but—"

"But you're not sure. Thank God," he said fervently, "that you're really learning—at last. Thank God you're really beginning to think—and to think round corners. Thank God you're looking for reasons—and for traps."

"I only hesitated because—"

"Because for a moment you had doubts about me. And why not? We met in peculiar circumstances and you knew—you still know—nothing whatsoever about me. But having doubted, look at the facts: at the time of your accident, I was two streets away, trying to reconcile a goat to the loss of her green pastures. Getting her along to the door and getting her through the doorway and into the house and out again and into the garden took time. Time and patience both. So you can rule me out. And having ruled me out, you can try and bring yourself to trust me. We both got anonymous letters—and now we've got to try and decide why they, whoever they are, wanted us to go to the Merlin Bar."

"Could Kennedy have sent the message?"

"We can find out."

He switched on the engine, and in silence they drove to the Dorset Court block of flats. They left the car almost exactly where it had been when Mr. Kennedy came out to speak to them; then they got out and entered the great building and made their way to the reception desk.

The clerk on duty was the one who had answered their questions about the tenants of Number Four. They had to wait a few moments for him to finish attending to two women. Then he came over to Jody and Desmond, bowed, smiled and announced himself at their service.

Could they, asked Desmond, speak to Mr. Kennedy?

There was at first a little confusion, but when the clerk understood the inquiry, he dealt with it clearly and intelligently. Nobody called Kennedy, he told them, had ever worked in the Reception Department or in any other capacity at Dorset Court. There was no post of Reception Manager and never had been. There were two clerks; himself and one other who was not short and stout, but tall and thin. Yes, Mr. and Mrs. Grierson had left hurriedly, as he told them when they made their previous inquiries—but not too hurriedly. The rent of the apartment had been paid in full, and the apartment itself left in excellent order.

Mrs. Grierson? Yes, she was a blonde, and goodlooking. Her Christian name? One could not say; one had never heard it; one regretted.

There was nothing further to be gained by prolonging the interview, nothing to be learned by further questioning. The man gave every indication of having answered frankly and fully. There was nothing to do but thank him—and leave.

"So where are we now?" inquired Jody, as they drove slowly away from the building.

"Exactly where we were. No; we're one yellow brick further back. At this rate," prophesied Desmond, "we'll soon discover that you had an accident one morning not so long ago." He brought the car to a stop at the traffic lights, and glanced at her. "Will you promise me one thing?"

"What is it?"

"Next time you get a message, anonymous or otherwise, you won't go off and investigate it alone."

"If you're going to get duplicates of the message, I won't be alone," she pointed out.

"Why didn't you tell anyone about it?"

"I read it in the train on my way up to London. I didn't see any point in ringing up Estelle or my aunt to tell them about it."

"You could and you should have told your brother-in-law."

"Well, I didn't tell him. And Charles is at Saint-Malo and so I couldn't tell him. What," she asked, "are we going to do now?"

"That depends on you," said Desmond. "We drop the whole thing now, or we go on. Myself, I'd like to catch up with these Griersons. Even more than that, I'd like to lay hands on the imaginative Mr. Kennedy. But you'll have to see how your family and your fiancé feel about it. I don't think they'll take kindly to your heading straight for trouble. My guess is that when you tell them what's happened today, they'll want you to pause and to ponder."

"I did pause and I did ponder. And now I'm not going to

pause and ponder any more. If there's a lead, I'm going to follow it, and I hope you are too. I'm sick to death," she said slowly, "of standing by and catching crumbs of clues as they're thrown to me. From now on, I'm going to try to find clues of my own—and if I find them, I'll follow them."

"I see. You know what that means?" he asked.

"Of course I know," said Jody. "We're in the detective business."

## CHAPTER
# 10

THEY DROVE DOWN TO Broome, both of them silent for the greater part of the journey. Desmond drove steadily, his eyes on the road; Jody did not know what he was thinking about, but she felt a curious sense of security. There had been a bridge between them and she had hesitated, for many reasons, to cross it. Now she was over it, and she had no regrets. Nor had she, she found, any of the doubts which had once been present in her mind. To tell Estelle and Michael? At present, no. She would speak to Charles when he returned from Saint-Malo. She would tell him everything that had happened, without reserve, and he would advise her as to how much it would be wise to tell the others.

Happiness filled her. She felt free and almost untroubled. She was no longer in this alone. Charles would support her and Desmond Huntley would encourage her, and if there were any more clues, they would unravel them together.

The car slowed, and Desmond nodded toward a quiet country hotel.

"Looks unpretentious," he said, "but you can get a wonderful dinner there. Tables out on a paved terrace, but not in the chilly night air—it's glassed-in and warm."

"Thank you all the same," said Jody, "but—"

"But no?"

"But no. Estelle's expecting me, and perhaps Charles will ring up from Saint-Malo, and I'm longing to talk to him."

"You're going to tell him?"

"When he gets back. But Estelle and Michael—not yet. If Michael thinks the school is going to be involved, he'll panic. Charles doesn't panic."

"Not about the school—but when he hears that you set off alone to the Merlin Bar, he isn't going to feel enthusiastic about the business."

"If you were a man and—"

"Which I trust I am."

"—and your fiancée had been lied to by fat men calling themselves Kennedy, and lured to a bar alone merely in order to catch sight of the same Kennedy leading away a woman who might or might not have been the woman he said he didn't know was who or where, then what would you say to her?"

"To the woman?"

"To your fiancée. Would you just say: 'I wouldn't take any notice, if I were you.' Would you?"

"Well, let's consider. I have this hypothetical fiancée, and so I love her. And so I want to protect her. And so . . . well," he mused, "I think I'd make her swear solemnly that she wouldn't make a move without me, and then—"

"And then?"

"Well, then I'd try to get a step further in the investigations. I wouldn't tell her everything I did, but I'd nose around Dorset Court seeing if I could catch a glimpse of Kennedy. I'd ask the waiters at the Merlin if they'd ever seen a quiet blonde in the bar before, and if so, with whom? I'd try to get into Number Four on some pretext or other and take a quick look at the carpet to see if it had recently been cleaned. But all that takes time, and didn't you say that Charles does a lot of coaching in between trips to sea?"

"Yes, he does."

"Even during the summer holidays?"

"Yes."

"If it isn't too impertinent a question—Why?" asked Desmond.

"Why does he do coaching? To make extra money. To make enough money to give up teaching."

"He doesn't like teaching?"

"He doesn't mind it, but it takes place indoors, and all he wants—all he's wanted all his life—is to be out, preferably on water. He was in the Navy once, but he got hurt in a skiing accident, and he's got a slight limp; you wouldn't notice it, but it's enough to keep him out of the service. He's saved up almost enough money but not quite enough to—"

"To free him?"

"Yes. And so he takes extra tutoring jobs when they're offered, and as soon as he can, he'll buy a boat large enough to live on fairly comfortably, and we'll get married and live on it. And that's why he's taken *Ballerina* to Saint-Malo—to try her out. If he likes her and if he and the Major agree about the price, Charles will buy her."

"The Major . . . is he on the school staff?"

"No. But he's helping Michael out and keeping the gardens tidy while the school gardeners are on holiday. That's why he's living in one of the school cottages. Normally, he lives in that little cottage above Marcove."

"And plays the violin?"

"Yes. Serious music with the Professor, or sea-chanties with the boys at the Tar Barrel. Nobody knows much about him, but Michael thinks he's all right."

"And do you?"

"I . . ." Jody hesitated. "I like him, but when he's talking to me, I find myself listening rather carefully with a view to catching him out. I try not to, but I can't help it. He talks an awful lot, and he talks very fast, and he's been everywhere and never seems to have been long in one place, and so after a time it gets rather confusing."

"Which you feel might be the object of the exercise?"

"Yes. But it's probably nothing but my imagination—If you put your foot on the accelerator," she broke off to add, "there'll be time for you to have a drink before dinner."

"I'm getting dinner?"

"Of course."

"Why of course? Your aunt—"

"—is an exception. Estelle will love to have you."

"And about this detective business?"

"Well?"

"Shall we call it Hern and Huntley?"

"Hern and Vaughan and Huntley."

"Not too cumbersome?"

"I don't think so."

"I detect," he said, "a cool note. The business note. In future, I take it, our meetings will be strictly unsocial, and our conversation confined to Kennedy?"

Jody turned her head and gave him a long and thoughtful look.

"You're trying to say something," she decided at last. "What, exactly?"

"I'm not trying to say anything. I'm merely trying to define my status in the firm, that's all."

"It's a threesome, and you're one-third of it."

"Suppose Charles has other ideas?"

"Such as what?" she asked.

He threw her an amused glance.

"Didn't anybody ever tell you that three was a crowd?"

"In business?"

"Ah, yes. I forgot we were in business. I'm a detective, not a man."

"And what," demanded Jody, "do you mean by that?"

He stopped the car in order to tell her.

"Why," he asked, turning to face her, "did you think I spent so many hours in your aunt's house, putting up with the zero treatment?"

"I'll tell you why," said Jody. "You're a naval man, which means you're an active man, and you're home on long leave, which means that you've got a lot of time on your hands. You meet a girl in rather unusual circumstances, which means that it seems to you more interesting to go clue-chasing than to do all the other things naval men like to do on leave. Which means—"

"Fate ties me up into your life, which means that I get a feeling of fatality, which means that I think about you as the girl who fainted right into my arms the very first time I saw her. Which means that you and I, whether we acknowledge it or not, have skipped a few of the usual preliminaries and are on firmly friendly terms. Are you receiving me, Miss Hern?"

"If you think Charles is idiotic enough to be jealous just because—"

"—I like you? I've never seen him," said Desmond, "but he sounds like a man who knows his own mind. If he's as level-headed as he sounds, he'll make it his business to keep Huntley away from Hern."

"If I assure him that the relationship between Hern and Huntley is entirely business-like—"

"And there," broke in Desmond pleasantly, "you can only speak for yourself, can't you?"

She stared at him.

"You mean," she said slowly, "that you're going to spoil a perfectly good detective business at the start by dragging in absurd complications?"

He laughed.

"Absurd? Did you ever, Miss Hern, take a good look at yourself?"

"I—"

"What do you see? I'll tell you. A small, slim, perfect figure. A small, tanned, oval face with eyes that go up a little, just a very little at the ends. A small, quite perfect nose. A skin you'd like—as the advertisements say—to touch. A mouth . . ." He stopped. "On the whole," he said, "I think Huntley resigns. He's a nice guy, Huntley; he hasn't any harm in him, but if Fate hands him the prettiest girl he's ever seen, he likes to feel he's got at least a lien on her. If somebody else got there first, he feels that the sensible thing to do, without delay, is to sign off. To pack up. To push off."

"You—"

"I said at the beginning of our acquaintance, if you remember, that I'd like to know whether this Vaughan knew what a prize he'd got. Well, I've given myself the answer. He doesn't know."

"You haven't the faintest right to—"

"He doesn't know. His interests are sailing, money-making and love, in that order."

Jody drew a deep, difficult breath.

"I should be glad," she said in a strangled voice, "if you would drive me home."

Without a word, he started the engine. Nothing whatsoever was said until he drew up before the house. Then he walked round and opened the door and assisted her out of the car.

"Goodbye," she said. "Thank you for driving me home."

He got into the car.

"The firm's dissolved?" he asked.

"Yes. I'm sorry," said Jody, "but after those things you said about Charles, you didn't really give me a choice, did you?"

He gave her a wide, engaging smile.

"Didn't I?"

The question hung in the air as he drove away. Jody stared after him for a moment, and then turned and went into the house. After trying one or two of the more likely rooms, she came upon Estelle in the kitchen.

"Hello, Jody. You're late, but it doesn't matter. We're alone."

"Where's Michael?"

"Playing in a darts match at the Tar Barrel. He's eating there."

"Fenella in bed?"

"No. Nancy Wigram came with her two boys this afternoon, and they all got on so well that she took Fenella back for the night. It's absolute heaven without her, just for once. Oh—Charles rang up from Saint-Malo. He wanted you, but I told him you were late and so he gave me the message."

"When is he leaving there?"

"He didn't say. But he's not coming back yet. The Cadmans are there and—"

"Cadmans?"

"You know—Mr. and Mrs., parents of the little Cadman boy who came last term. They're over at Saint-Malo with a boat like *Ballerina* and Charles thinks he might be able to get it for less money."

"I see," said Jody slowly. "And what about his message?"

"I wrote down a list of pupils he gave me. He says will you ring them all up and tell them he's got stuck over there and can't get back. He said ringing up from here would be cheaper than sending telegrams from there. I'm getting a cold supper—all right?"

"All right. I'll put these phone calls through first," said Jody.

She went into the hall, a sense of oppression weighing her footsteps. It stayed with her as she put through the four calls and made excuses to four strangers at the other end of the wire. Then she walked over to the open front door and stood staring out across the lawns, her mind blank and heavy. She could see, seated in the little drawing room of his cottage, the Professor, bent over—she guessed—a manuscript. In her tiny front garden next door, Miss Bishop bent over weeds. In the third cottage Jody could see the Major through his open window, seated in a deep chair, reading. The three made a picture of peace and, thought Jody a sort of coziness. Domestic comfort. The quiet evening, and people in their homes, working or reading, just being quiet and . . . at home.

Home. It was a nice word. A home of one's own. Perhaps this depression settling on her was caused less by the disappointment of not having Charles here than by the sight of those cottages and the picture of tranquillity within.

And then, examining her feelings, Jody found that she did not feel disappointed, or homeless. All she felt was a vast, terrifying loneliness.

She was alone. And perhaps it was her own fault. If she

had taken Charles into her confidence from the first moment, perhaps he would not now be across the Channel, thinking of everything but herself. Desmond Huntley had offered a hand and perhaps she had too hastily brushed it aside. Nothing he had said need have been treated seriously. He had gone a little too far, but she should have behaved like an adult and ordered him back across the line, instead of stepping out of his car with a haughty air and dismissing him.

Hern and Vaughan and Huntley. Huntley was gone. Vaughan was attending to his own affairs. Hern . . .

She heard the sound of a car, and looked up to see Desmond Huntley negotiating the last curve of the drive and stopping before the door. So great was her surprise, so swift his arrival that she had no time to analyze the bound that her heart gave. She took a step forward, and then he was out of the car and standing before her.

"Huntley, with apologies," he said. "First for being a fool and next for being selfish. There's only one important matter before the board at this moment, and that's the Grierson mystery. We could have made a good team, the three of us, and I'm here to bite the dust and ask you to forgive me."

To her bitter humiliation, she felt two tears welling from her eyes and rolling down her cheeks. He caught one of them on a large forefinger and held it up for her inspection and spoke in a speculative tone.

"Dew?" he inquired gently.

"I'm . . . I'm being s-stupid," she said unsteadily. "It's because I'm sorry for having been so selfish."

"Selfish? You?"

"Yes. You're on leave, and you could have been having such fun, and I took it for granted that all you wanted to do was get mixed up in a lot of things that probably have quite a simple explanation, once you got them cleared up. You could have been—"

"—popping up bars and wasting petrol and enriching nightclubs? I suppose I could. How about a junior partnership?"

"We'd like to have you."

"Good. And now how about dinner? If there isn't enough for me, why don't we all go out and eat somewhere?"

"No. It's nicer here. I'll go and talk to Estelle."

She went into the kitchen and spoke briefly and to the point.

"Desmond Huntley's here and he wants dinner. Can he stay?"

"Of course he can stay. But . . . didn't he drive you home?"

"Yes."

"And then he went away?"

"Yes."

"And then he came back?"

"Yes."

"What's going on?" asked Estelle slowly.

"Nothing's going on. What's for dinner?"

"Cold chops and salad and cheese and biscuits and coffee. That can't possibly fill a man of his size. You'd better—"

"I'll go and call him," said Jody.

CHAPTER

# 11

On the following day Jody lunched with her aunt. She found the house restored to its former immaculateness and its owner her normal, poised self.

"Did you tell Clarice?" she asked.

"I certainly did not." Lady Cleeve sounded surprised. "I told her nothing. What could she have done except worry?"

"Two pokers are better—"

"I know, I know. You said that before. Why couldn't you come to dinner with me tonight, as I asked you? Lunch gives us no time to chat."

"I wanted to get home in good time. I'm going out to Marcove."

"To Marcove? Didn't you tell me that Charles was away?"

"Yes. But Estelle and Michael and I are going down after dinner to arrange about a berth for a boat."

"Whose boat?"

"Desmond Huntley's."

"He's going to keep a boat at Marcove?"

"Yes."

"I see. How much," inquired Lady Cleeve, "do Estelle and her husband know about him—and you?"

"As much as is good for them," answered Jody. "When Charles gets back, I'm going to tell him the whole thing."

"He chose a bad time," said Lady Cleeve sagely, "not to be here. Are you sure you know what you're doing?"

"In the sense you mean it," said Jody, "I'm not doing anything."

"Odd, isn't it?" mused Lady Cleeve. "People always dissociate themselves from circumstances. If you saw another girl with an absent fiancé filling in her time with a rather attractive newcomer, what would you say to her?"

"I did better than that. I said it to the newcomer."

"Really?" Lady Cleeve's voice expressed only polite inter-

111

est. "And he, of course, explained hastily that he wasn't that kind of man?"

"He did better than that. He proved it. He dined with Estelle and myself last night. He was amusing and interesting, and he made himself useful, and—"

"—and made sure that he made a rendezvous for the next evening before he left?"

"Wrong. Estelle made it. He told her about the boat, and she said she'd ask Michael to fix up a berth. And that's all."

"Are you expecting me to swallow all this with my salad, Jody?"

Jody laughed.

"I'm trying to allay your suspicions. Everything's all right. When Charles comes back, he and Desmond Huntley and I are going to look into every detail of that accident of mine and really face facts instead of trying to dodge them. The accident, and the Griersons, and Laurie and the mysterious Mr. Kennedy . . . and an anonymous letter and a visit to a place called the Merlin Bar."

Lady Cleeve listened to the details in silence.

"But Jody I . . . I don't like it."

"I don't think I like it much, either," confessed Jody. "All I'm certain of is that you can get tired of nibbling at the edge of a puzzle. If I get a chance to bite off a bit more, I'm going to take it. Flanked, of course, by Charles and Desmond. Would you like to run into either of them when they were in a fighting mood?"

"Frankly, no. Jody . . . be careful."

"Of course!" Jody came round the table and dropped a kiss on her aunt's cheek. "Of course I'll be careful."

When she came out of the office that evening, she found Desmond Huntley's car parked outside and its owner seated at the wheel reading an evening paper. She hesitated for a moment before she went up to him, testing her own reactions. Surprise and pleasure at seeing him, and relief at not having to make the journey by train, were the only emotions she could recognize.

He came round and opened the door.

"I happened to be in town," he said, "and it's a nice day for a run."

"It's heavenly." Jody got in and settled herself on the deep cushions. "What have you been doing all day?"

"Amusing your niece and my nephews."

"Is Fenella home again?"

"She will be by the time we get back." He turned the car into the slow line of traffic in Piccadilly and spoke evenly. "Why didn't you tell me that Charles was staying on at Saint-Malo?"

"After all the harsh things you said about him," said Jody, "I didn't want you to think he'd run out on me. Who told you?"

"My sister."

"And Estelle told her. How fast can this car go on an open road?"

He showed her, and they got home in time for Jody to go upstairs and see Fenella into bed. She found her more agreeable than she had been since the departure of her brothers to the camp, and it did not take Jody long to find out why: her niece had made an important discovery. Not all boys, she had learned at the Wigrams, were like her brothers. Not all boys returned evil for evil with sickening promptitude and success. There were other modes, other codes.

"Sissies!" she hissed to her aunt, as clearly as a mouthful of toothpaste would allow.

"Who?"

"Julian and Piers Wigram."

"I'm sure they're not sissies. Brush your back teeth."

"What for brush them? Nobody can see those ones."

"Do you want them to go bad?"

"I'll get new ones, like the boys."

"And in the meantime, you'll clean the old ones. Hurry up."

"Sissies," repeated Fenella, stepping into her bath. "Why can't I have a barf with nothing on with Julian and Piers, same's with the twins?"

"Because brothers are brothers. Shut your eyes, or they'll get soap in them."

Fenella shut her eyes but opened her mouth to speak, and a small disturbance followed. When it was over, she reverted to the subject uppermost in her mind.

"They're sissies," she said. "I kicked them, and they didn't kick me."

"You what?"

"I kicked them."

"Well, I hope they jolly well kicked you back—hard."

Fenella shook her head—a long, satisfied movement that went on for some time.

"No. They couldn't," she explained at last.

"Why couldn't they?"

"Cos their mummy wouldn't let them."

"Well, when I've had a little talk with her, she'll let them."

"Don't you!" shouted Fenella, her face scarlet with rage. "Don't you tell them! Their mummy said they couldn't kick back. She said that! She said they had to be . . . to be gennelmen. She said so!"

Jody unwrapped the small form from the enormous towel and put it into a pair of pajamas.

"Bed," she said. "No gentleman has to stand still while you kick him."

"He can run away."

"And if he does, you know what happens? You kick him again, next time he shows up."

"Next time he—"

"—puts in an apperance. That's why your brothers kick you back—to show you what it feels like. If they didn't do that, you'd go right through life until you were a big girl, just kicking people and not knowing what it felt like to be kicked back."

"I do know what it feels like. It feels hurting, and that's why I—"

"That's why you prefer all the kicking to be on one side? I'm sure you would. Prayers. Keep your feet for dancing and not for kicking. Come on, prayers."

"'Please God let me be a good girl,'" prayed Fenella without warmth. "'And bless Julian and Piers, A-men.'"

"How about Mummy and Daddy and the boys—and me?"

"I said that inside. Kiss me good night."

Jody kissed her, tucked her in and went downstairs. Estelle came into the kitchen and helped her with the preparations for dinner; as usual, Jody found her little help but good company.

And as always, when she sat between Estelle and Michael at the long gleaming table in the dining room and looked at her brother-in-law's handsome head silhouetted against the lovely windows, she felt a sense of pleasure and pride. Their mode of living was simple, even Spartan, but they lived in beauty. They rose in the morning in beautiful rooms, and if they were ice-cold in winter, at this time of the year one forgot the winter's discomfort. They ate in gracious surroundings, and if the great fireplace yawned vast and half-empty in winter, now it could be looked at and fuel bills forgotten.

Tonight, Desmond Huntley sat opposite to her instead of Charles. Michael, who could at dinner be withdrawn, depressed or brooding, according to the day's effect upon him, tonight elected to be friendly; his manner was the one Jody liked to think of as his natural one: easy, relaxed and charming. As always, she had no idea what he was thinking, but his manner toward the guest left nothing to be desired. The scene, she reflected, was almost perfect, and she knew that she was the only one in the room who regretted Charles's absence.

Desmond was talking of television.

"Is there a set for the boys?"

"One? Almost every boy," said Michael, "arrives with his own portable set."

"And glues his nose to it every evening?"

"It's a gamble," said Michael. "The staff see to it that every time the programs offer something special in the way of trash, there's something interesting to do or to see elsewhere. It's a sort of game, and sometimes a rewarding one."

"How long have you been running the school?" asked Desmond.

"Ten and a half years. I always liked the place. The school itself was once an abbey."

"And according to one bright pupil's essay," said Estelle, "it dissolved in 1536. All that didn't dissolve were the four walls."

"That was when this house was built—on the foundations of an older one," said Michael. "They used a lot of stone from the dissolved abbey. Then the abbey rose again as a priest's college, and in time fell into disrepair again, and was eventually rebuilt and turned into a school. I don't suppose I would have bought it if my wife hadn't fallen in love with this house."

Desmond was looking across the lawns.

"Why are those three cottages so close to the house?" he asked.

"Wartime erections. If the British had had the place, they would have put up huts, but the Americans were here, and they amused themselves by building those three genuine reproductions. I was so glad to have them as staff cottages that I left them there. I'm growing a few trees to keep them out of sight, but as you see, trees have a hard job to get a start here; we're so exposed that the young ones either get blown down or uprooted. The Major's giving his mind to the problem."

"What can't the Major do?" asked Jody.

"I haven't found out yet," said Michael.

"How long has he been here?" asked Desmond.

"About a year," Michael told him. "He seems to be getting a bit restless again; he's like the trees; can't get his roots down. Jody, that was a nice dinner. But if my guess is correct, we're not going to get out to Marcove. Rain."

She looked out with an unexpectedly sharp feeling of disappointment creeping over her. She had been looking forward to going, she hardly knew why. A drive to Marcove was scarcely to be counted as a treat. But she saw the drizzle increasing and becoming heavier, and soon gusts of wind were bending the trees and the drizzle had become a downpour.

"So what?" asked Michael. "Game of bridge?"

Desmond looked at Estelle.

"Perhaps you'd play for us," he suggested.

They went into the drawing room. Estelle played, at first for the others and then, forgetting them, for herself. Michael rose and wandered away to his study, and Jody and Desmond sat on in their deep chairs, saying nothing, listening or half-listening to the music.

When the rain stopped, it was almost dark, and too late to go to Marcove. Desmond took his leave, and Jody walked out into the hall to see him off. The door, as always on summer evenings, stood open, and in the half-light the sodden lawns looked black. From the three cottages twinkled lights, all on the ground floor; nobody had gone to bed.

"Pity about the Cove," said Desmond. "Tomorrow?"

"Yes. Or we could wait until Charles gets back," said Jody.

He said nothing, but he noted the wind's increasing force. He looked across at the dark school building.

"It looks like an abbey now," he said.

"It always does in this light. And at night, if we have to

go over to the school for anything—during the holidays, I mean—it's nice and ghosty."

"You like ghosts?"

"Ghosts of monks, yes. One of them's supposed to walk up and down the terrace on the other side of the building."

"Have you seen him?"

"No. But I've often looked."

"Let's look now. He might have come out to sniff the nice washed air."

She laughed, and they walked by wet paths across to the school and through an archway to its far side. Here the sense of being deep in the country vanished; all was open, treeless, exposed, and at intervals could be heard the thunder of surf. The wind was still rising, and Jody's hair was blown wildly round her face.

"No monk," she said, "would want to walk in this."

"No wonder the school has such a wonderful health record," commented Desmond. "The boys are either blown away and never heard of again, or they breathe this air and thrive." The wind gave a playful push, and he held Jody's arm. "Steady," he said. "I think I'll get you indoors again."

They turned to face the wind, and fought their way back to the archway; then they stood to regain their breath.

"Storm?" she asked.

"Yes. But you needn't worry about Charles; he'll be safe at Saint-Malo, and he won't attempt to cross in this. That's the worst of a trip across the Channel; you might get back on schedule, or you might not—and usually you don't. Hang onto me, and we'll make for the front door again. No we won't," he corrected himself, "we'll wait for this shower to stop."

The shower did not stop for some time, but neither of them was in a hurry; both were enjoying the wild weather, stepping swiftly out of the way of windborne spray that dashed into the entrance of the archway, bracing themselves against the mounting fury of the wind.

In time, the rain lessened to a light fall; laughing, hand-in-hand, they chose a moment between gusts of wind and ran toward the house. Then he said goodbye to her, and drove away, and she locked the front door and walked slowly upstairs. She reached the gallery and switched on the lights and stood watching the moon emerging from the clouds and throwing its light on the wet lawns before being smothered once more in a soft black veil.

She felt the chill of the house striking through her damp dress, but she did not move. Head against a window pane, like an imprisoned child gazing at the world outside, she stood with her eyes going slowly over the familiar scene: the cottages, still with their lights burning in the lower windows, the silhouette of the school buildings. She was not thinking, tonight, of the gallery ghosts; her thoughts were of today and of tomorrow.

She turned at last to go to her room, and groped for gallery light. Then she paused, wondering if her ears were deceiving her, for she felt sure that she had heard the sound of a car's engine starting.

Her first thought was that Desmond had returned, failed to see her and was going away again. But as she turned once more to the window, she saw, moving very slowly, the outline of a car—and it was not Desmond's.

She waited for its lights to flash out, but no lights appeared. Very slowly, as though the driver was feeling a way along the dark, curving drive, the car inched forward.

The next few moments were never clear in her mind. She was running downstairs; she had opened the front door and was speeding across the grass, as she or Estelle had sped a hundred times to stop Michael's car, or Charles's, to give a forgotten message or hand in a forgotten article. A short cut took them to a point further down the drive; if they were lucky, they reached it seconds before the car.

And now Jody was running, but she did not know what she was going to do if she saw the car. She knew only that for one short moment she had, by the light of the moon, caught a glimpse of the driver's head, and had sensed rather than seen something familiar. She might be crazy, she told herself as she raced, . . . but she had to know.

She was too late. As she emerged, panting, from the bushes bordering the drive, the car went by. Its speed had quickened, and its lights were on. A moment, and it had vanished round another curve.

But she had seen, in that moment, what she had come to see. She had proved what she had come to prove.

The man in the car was Mr. Kennedy.

## CHAPTER
# 12

"And he didn't see you?" asked Desmond.

"No."

"You're absolutely certain?"

"Absolutely."

"And you didn't have time to see even one figure of the car number?"

"I . . . I didn't even think of looking," confessed Jody. "I wasn't thinking at all. But when the car had gone, I went back to the house and knocked on Estelle's door. I went in, and I think they thought I was out of my mind. I was wet, and they hadn't any idea you'd stayed so long after saying goodbye to them, and I must have looked crazy."

"And they didn't know anything about him?"

"Not a thing. I said I'd seen a man called Kennedy driving away. They waited; they were both quite blank-looking and I'm quite certain neither of them had the slightest idea who or what I was talking about."

"And then?"

"And then Estelle asked who this Mr. Kennedy was. I said that he posed as the Reception Manager at Dorset Court."

"And then?"

"And then Michael looked at his watch and saw what the time was and realized that I was walking about, wet, in their bedroom talking about people in cars, when it was obvious that anybody, whether I knew them or not, could have been calling on the Professor or the Major or Miss Bishop. He asked what all the fuss was about, and he didn't ask politely, and then he blasted me out of the room. And I went away feeling I'd been a fool not to have waited until the morning, but . . . but I'm certain that I wasn't mistaken about the man in the car. It was Mr. Kennedy."

Desmond said nothing. They were lunching together; she had telephoned during the morning and they had met in order to talk over the new development. The restaurant in Soho, not far from her office, was crowded; people came and went, but to the two at their corner table, the place might have been empty. They sat on for a while in silence, their meal over but their conclusions no further advanced.

"When I decided to become a detective," said Desmond broodingly, "I imagined myself sifting the evidence for six seconds and then coming out with a masterly piece of deduction."

"So did I."

"But what can anybody do with evidence of this kind? I daresay old Sherlock Holmes would have taken one look at Kennedy and told his stooge Watson exactly who and what he was, and also where he came from. But for myself, I didn't notice anything beyond the fact that he was short and fat and out of condition. He said he was a Reception Manager and that's what he looked like. I suppose I ought to have taken a closer look when he started throwing out hints about blood—but how was anybody to know that he wasn't a Reception Manager and had nothing to do with Dorset Court and knew perfectly well where to find Laurie and—"

"Not necessarily. Why couldn't he have sent those anonymous letters himself? He gets us to the Merlin Bar and we see him with Laurie; that might have been his way of letting us know that he'd found her."

"And he took her away like that because he didn't want to give us time to speak to her—is that it?"

"Could be."

"All right; so he's found her. So who steals papers from your aunt's flat? And why do they all relate to you? And why does Kennedy drive away without lights from the school at midnight? If he was visiting someone in one of those three cottages, wouldn't he just drive away like anybody else, with a couple of door bangings and a bit of revving as he goes off? Why sneak out? Everybody was up; you'd only just put the hall light out."

"Do you think he knew you were there?"

"He knows my car, and my car was parked in the drive—but it wasn't there when he came out, if he was in one of the cottages. So why the caution?"

"The next thing is to ask the Professor and the Major and Miss Bishop if they know a man called Kennedy," said Jody.

"You mean you'll pay a visit to each of them this evening?"

"I won't have to go to them. They're coming over for a practice. Why don't you come? I could ask them and you could watch to see if any of them tried to be evasive."

Desmond looked apprehensive.

"They'd be playing that music again, wouldn't they?"

"Yes. It's good music."

"It's murder. But I'll come. And we'll ask the Trio if they know Kennedy."

"But if they say they've never heard of him, we're no further on."

"Aren't we? A man drives away at midnight. We didn't see his car, so he couldn't have left it where a visitor would normally leave it—on the drive."

"No. It was parked out of sight, where the drive comes round by the Major's cottage."

"He hides his car. And he drives away with as little noise as possible."

"Could he have had a midnight appointment with someone? Could he have driven up, seen your car, waited until you were out of the way and then gone away?"

"Why would he go away? He might wait until I'd gone, but once I'd gone, he'd pay his visit, wouldn't he?"

"Could he . . ." Jody hesitated.

"Could he what?"

"Could he have been watching us?"

Desmond stared at her, and the color rose in her cheeks.

"What in the world," he asked slowly, "would he do that for?"

"I . . . I don't know. But he saw us together, and came out and spoke to us. He sent both of us anonymous letters."

"If he sent them at all."

"If he sent them at all. The first evening you dine with us, he appears. Why?"

"I thought you were on the point of telling me."

She looked dejected.

"So we ask the Trio about him?"

"We do. And if they say they've never heard of him, we can be sure of something we're sure of already."

"Which is?"

"Which is that something's going on. I don't think Kennedy was there to hide behind a bush and peer at us. I think he was there to see somebody. Where are you going?"

"Back to work, of course. I've got an appointment for three o'clock."

He rose and stood looking down at her.

"I wish," he said, "that you were free all day."

She laughed.

"So do I."

"If it isn't inquiring too freely into what isn't my business, could I know why a girl with, I gather from one or two things your aunt said, money coming in on her next birthday, and a wedding coming off in the foreseeable future—"

"—takes a job in London and does a tedious journey to and fro every day? The money's coming, but it hasn't come. I do enough for my sister to enable me to live on her without too many qualms, but I like my job and I like having my own spending money. And I like the change from town to country every day. And I like the feeling of doing just a bit more than I can manage; it keeps me moving, and I like moving. Aunt Essie doesn't understand that; she likes what she calls leisure, which means time to think of a way to kill time."

He drove her to the office, and told her that he would be waiting for her, and watched her as she walked away from the car. The wind, high and getting higher, tore at her dress and at the scarf she had tied round her hair, and he remembered the weather report and the prospect of further gales, and was glad. Charles Vaughan was stuck at Saint-Malo, and it served him right for being too obtuse to see that an accident was not necessarily an accident. Blow, winds, blow.

Then he saw that she had turned and was coming back.

"When you're not at your sister's cottage," she asked, "where are you?"

"You mean you care?"

"I mean I'd like to know. If I hadn't found you at home this morning when I rang you up, where could I have found you to tell you about Mr. Kennedy and the car?"

He brought out a card and scribbled a line on it.

"Phone number of my club," he said. "If I move around, I'll tell Nancy or the hall porter where you can get hold of me."

Jody put the card into her handbag, and went into the building with a peculiar feeling of satisfaction. She could find him—if she wanted to. He would be available—if she needed him. She wouldn't, she told herself, want to find him, and she certainly wouldn't need him, but odd things were happening, and if Mr. Kennedy turned up again, she would feel happier to know that Desmond was at hand.

He was waiting for her when she came out, and it seemed natural that he should be there, ready to fold up his newspaper when she appeared, opening the door, handing her in, pausing before they drove away in order to tuck in the strands of hair that had escaped from her scraf.

"It's still terribly wind," she said. "I rang Estelle; there's been no word of Charles."

"If he attempts the crossing in weather like this," said Desmond, "he'll be crazy."

But a man in love, he reflected, was crazy. Even so, no small boat could cross the Channel in weather like this. And so one man in love must wait in France, and another man in love might seize the chance that Fate and the weather had given him. Nobody wanted to take a mean advantage of a man who couldn't be present to keep an eye on his girl—but there were certain unusual aspects about this engagement which gave outsiders an idea that the tie was anything but a strong one. If this girl sitting beside him now was in love, deeply and passionately, he was prepared to eat the ends of the heavy silk scraf that was blowing in his face. If the word "unawakened" meant anything, it could be applied to the girl in this case. Of the man he knew nothing beyond the fact that he had failed to help the girl he loved over a sticky patch. She had been afraid, and a man in love, if he was worth anything, didn't dismiss the fears, tell her to think about something else, and go sailing.

On the other hand, a fellow who came along and undermined another fellow's prospects when the other fellow was out of the way . . .

"What are you thinking about?" Jody asked.

"You and your fiancé."

"Oh."

The sound was noncommittal, and he said no more. If she wanted to know any more, she would ask—and he would answer. But she did not ask.

"Tell me," she said instead, "about yourself."

"About me? I told you. I told you and your aunt that first evening. Age—"

"Not those things. Other things. Where were you born?"

"India. My parents were among the very last batch of

what used to be called Empire-builders. Dartmouth at thirteen and a half, and then the usual things: Greenwich, at sea, courses, at sea, more courses and more at sea. Exciting, isn't it? How about you?"

"Even more exciting. School, another school, yet another school—a job, another job, yet another job—and now this job."

"Did your aunt bring you and your sister up?"

"Yes. She had a house in Kent—a nice one, with a garden and an orchard and paddock. When Estelle married and I left school for good, she sold the big house and bought herself the little one in London."

"And how did men ever get near you or Estelle? If they got the ice treatment—"

"She doesn't like them herself," explained Jody, "but she tries to be reasonable and admit that other women might have different ideas. Like all relations, she wouldn't have chosen the men we chose. She never got on with Michael, and she doesn't really get on with Charles."

"And they care?"

"Charles doesn't. He can't bear her. Michael would like her to come down more often in term time; he thinks she has publicity value."

There was a lot of Charles in the conversation, mused Desmond. But a man had to be thankful for what he'd got—and he had a lot at this moment. Jody beside him. An evening with Jody ahead of him. Blow, oh winds, and keep on blowing.

They got home to find Miss Bishop alone in the drawing room. She was seated at a small table, copying out a sheet of music. The Major and the Professor, she explained, would be here soon, and then all three of them would begin to practice.

"We all had an early dinner," she said, "and then I came over to get this last piece of music copied out for the Professor."

"I saw Mr. Kennedy driving away from the cottages last night," said Jody. "I had no idea he knew anybody down here. Was it you he had been to see?"

Miss Bishop, pen poised, raised her sensible brown eyes to Jody's. She seemed to hesitate before speaking, but her answer, when it came, was calm enough.

"Mr. Kennedy? I don't think I know anybody called Kennedy," she said. "Certainly nobody come to see me last night."

She seemed about to say more, but the door opened and the Major entered, in one hand his violin case and in the other a large basket of vegetables. Having put down the violin, he followed Jody out to the kitchen.

"Seemed a pity not to pick all this greenery," he said. "The stuff shouldn't be allowed to go to waste. I'll take a load into the village tomorrow and turn it into money; I wonder the Headmaster doesn't do it more often."

Jody put the vegetables on to a rack and returned the empty basket.

"You don't," she asked, "happen to know anybody called Kennedy?"

When she had had more experience as an investigator, she reflected, she would know better than to put a leading question to somebody who had his back turned toward her and who had ample time, before opening the kitchen door, to conceal any emotions the question might have raised.

"Kennedy? Kennedy?" The Major turned from the door and, head on one side, considered the question. "Yes. Know two Kennedys, as a matter of fact. One out in Rhodesia; nice chap. Married a French girl. C. W. Kennedy, he was. That the one you mean?"

"Well, I thought I saw a Mr. Kennedy driving away last night and—"

"Couldn't have been C. W. Know for a fact he's still out there. Only other Kennedy I know is old Freddy Kennedy who runs a sort of fruit farm down in Kent. Getting past it a bit, I tell him; he must be rising seventy, but he's still active enough. Still, his wife's a good deal younger, and I think she does a lot of the grind. Funny; when they married, you'd have thought she couldn't have stood the life; delicate, she was. Wispy little thing. She—"

"I only wondered whether—"

"She was musical, too. That's how I got to know 'em. She heard I could play the fiddle, and she—"

"I only thought that parhaps Mr. Kennedy—the Mr. Kennedy I know—had been visiting you last night."

"Visiting me? Not me," said the Major. "C. W.'s in Rhodesia, and old Freddy's spending a month with his sister up in Bute. Got a card from him the other day saying his wife was to join them next week, and wanted to know if I'd go too.

Said no, of course; told him I couldn't abandon my post here until the gardeners got back. Well, I'll leave you; I know you're anxious to get dinner ready. Had a couple of chops early; the Professor's keen to get in a long practice."

The Professor arrived at the same time as Michael and Estelle and Fenella, who had been out. They met in the hall; Michael hoisted Fenella onto his shoulder and took her upstairs to get ready for bed, and the Professor carried Estelle's parcels to the kitchen.

"Sorry we're late, Jody." She turned to smile at Desmond as he came in. "We did an afternoon's shopping, and then we went to call on your sister," she told him.

"If I'd known, Jody and I would have looked in on our way back," he said.

"He's staying to dinner, Estelle. Is that all right?" asked Jody.

"That's lovely." Estelle turned him toward the door. "Go with the Professor to the drawing room and when Jody and I are ready, we'll come in and then we can all have a drink. Professor, go along; you can't begin playing until you've had something to drink."

"I like that 'Jody and I' touch," commented Jody, when they had gone. "You made it sound as though you really worked."

"Well, I'm here; give me a job."

"You can make the salad."

Estelle began the preparations, forgot what she was doing and sat on the edge of the table to talk.

"I like those Wigrams, Jody. They're nice. She's smart without being too dressy, and he's talkative in a nice interesting way—not like the Major. We all tried to fly kites, but it was too gusty."

"Did Fenella kick the boys?"

"I didn't notice. Nancy Wigram was asking me about you. She's interested in you. She said you're the first girl she's ever seen her brother take a real interest in, and she wishes he'd met you sooner." She paused. "In a way, so do I. Oh, and that reminds me, Jody. Charles rang up."

Jody turned.

"What did he say?"

"He said the weather reports are good, and he's coming back with the Cadmans to Newhaven."

"Why Newhaven?"

"That's where they keep their boat. He's bought it."

"Bought it?" echoed Jody in surprise. "Not *Ballerina?*"

"No. He'll sail *Ballerina* back to Marcove when he's fixed up all the business with the Cadmans."

"I see. When does he expect to get back?"

"With luck, he says, the day after tomorrow, early in the morning. Didn't you give me a job to do?"

"The salad."

"Oh. Well, before I do it, I'd better do Fenella's supper. She's coming down when she's undressed."

"There's her cereal in the jar behind you—in that cupboard. The milk's warming and I've put out a piece of the plain cake. Don't let her eat it in here, Estelle; I want to work fast, and I can't if she's around. Take it into the drawing room, and I'll come when I'm ready."

When she went, some time later, to the drawing room, Estelle was alone, seated at the piano and playing softly, dinner and preparations for dinner forgotten. Jody walked up to her and leaned against the instrument, listening and watching the beautiful hands moving on the keyboard.

There was silence when the music came to an end.

"Nice," said Jody at last. "Debussy?"

"Yes. But I meant to go and help you."

"It's all right; it's done. Where's everybody?"

"The Professor's with Miss Bishop in the study. The Major went back to fetch his music. Michael and Desmond walked over to look at the cottages—and here they come."

"And Fenella?"

"Fenella? Oh!" Estelle rose and gazed distractedly round the room. "She went to hide—I was supposed to count twenty and then go and find her."

A wild shriek from Fenella and a series of Indian war cries from Miss Bishop indicated that somebody else had been found for the game. The door burst open and Fenella rushed into the room, followed by Miss Bishop, and the two circled the sofa at high speed.

"Hey!" Michael, ushering Desmond in by the other door, caught his daughter up in his arms. "Hey, there. Time for Miss Bishop to have a drink. Where's the Professor?"

"He's trying over a piece of music in the study," said Miss Bishop. "I don't think he wants a drink."

"He won't refuse a brandy," said Michael, pouring it out and handing the glass to Jody. "Take that to him," he said.

Jody carried it to the study and Miss Bishop went with her. The Professor, cello between his knees and the sheet of music laid on a table by his side, was plucking softly at the strings and peering shortsightedly at the notes. Miss Bishop walked over and stood beside him.

"All right?" she asked, with a nod toward the music.

He looked at her with his characteristic blank, unseeing gaze and then seemed to become aware that he was being spoken to.

"Please?"

"The music" Miss Bishop pointed. "Any mistakes?"

"Oh. The music. No, no, no, no—no mistakes," he assured her. "No mistakes. Everything is very good. You are very kind."

"Brandy—from the Headmaster," said Jody, handing him the glass.

"This is for me?"

"Yes."

"Oh! How kind! That is so kind!" The Professor waved the glass gently under his nose. "Ah! It is good!"

"Come and have it with the rest of us in the drawing room," urged Jody.

"Thank you—no." The Professor gave a vague glance at the music. "I have just to practice a little before—"

"Nonsense, Professor," broke in Miss Bishop heartily. "It'll take exactly five minutes, and then you can come back here. Be sociable!"

The Professor, unwilling, reluctant, was shepherded to the door. He waited for Jody, and as Miss Bishop walked ahead and went out of earshot, she found time to ask him a question. She had to ask it more than once; when at last he understood what she wanted to know, he told her that he knew no Kennedys. He said that he had not heard the name before, asked how it was spelled, and thought that he had once met some English people called Kendy. On the other hand, he might be mistaking them for a German family he had once met; they were called Kondi. No, no, no; so stupid; the Kondis were not German at all. They were—

With relief, Jody entered the drawing room, and the Professor was claimed by Estelle. Desmond came over to join her bringing his drink and hers, and drew her to the window, where he could speak to her without being overheard by the others.

"Huntley reporting to Hern," he said.

She looked up at him.

"Reporting?"

"I asked your brother-in-law to show me those three cottages. It was wet last night and the ground's sodden and I thought I might be able to see footprints—and see where they led."

"And did you?"

"Not one. Whoever came last night walked unswervingly along the paths. Is that any way for intruders to behave? What chance does it give a detective?"

"From what I've seen of Mr. Kennedy," said Jody thoughtfully, "he wouldn't be so obliging as to strew clues around. But whether his footprints were there or not—he was."

Fenella scrambled by, her game with Miss Bishop renewed. The two went out of the room and were heard chasing one another round the hall.

"Jody—dinner, I think," said Estelle. "I'll tell Fenella to go to bed."

"One more drink," said Michael.

The Professor said that he ought to go back to the study, but on seeing Miss Bishop still engaged at hide-and-seek with Fenella, accepted another brandy.

"After this," he asked them, "how shall I play? Always I take nothing, and tonight, I have two glasses full." He turned the drink slowly in his hand, and turned blue, appreciative eyes on Michael. "It is good," he said. "It is very, very good."

Jody smiled at him as she went to the door.

"I'm going to see to the dinner, but you're not to hurry," she said. "There's heaps of time."

"I'm coming with you," said Desmond. "I'm the best disher-upper in the county."

He closed the door behind them and they went toward the kitchen.

"Tell me again," said Jody, "about the footprints. You went to look at the cottages, and—"

Her words and her steps came to an abrupt halt. Desmond, turning in surprise, retraced his steps and came to stand beside her.

"What's up?" he asked.

Jody did not answer. Leaning against one of the long windows, trying in vain to screen herself from their view, stood Miss Bishop. One hand was held against her heart, and her face was deathly white.

In a moment, Jody and Desmond were beside her.

"What is it? What is it, Miss Bishop?" Jody put an arm round her shoulders and attempted to lead her toward the drawing room, only to find Miss Bishop resisting strongly.

"No . . . no." The words came in a gasp. "I'm . . . I'll be . . . all right. I . . ."

Jody glanced at Desmond.

"Will you call Estelle?" she asked him.

"No—no!" Miss Bishop's voice was strangled. She put out a hand and made a frenzied clutch at Desmond's arm. "No!"

Jody supported the stout, shaking form as well as she could, and in a few moments, to her relief, saw a faint color return to the ashen cheeks.

"Please let me send for something—anything," she begged gently. "You played too long with Fenella, and you've overdone it. Let me—"

"Yes." Miss Bishop fought desperately to regain her self-command. "Yes. I . . . was very foolish. I . . ."

"If you'll sit down for a little while—"

"No. No, not here. If you'll . . . if you'll let me go into the kitchen with you while I . . . while I . . . Please . . ."

Between them, they supported her to the kitchen and put her into a chair. Jody knelt beside her, saying nothing, holding the trembling hands and chafing them gently. The moments passed, and gradually the trembling ceased. Then Miss Bishop drew a deep breath, looked from one to the other and spoke shakily.

"Thank you. Thank you both. That was . . . just what I need. You've very kind."

"Won't you take something? A drink?" asked Desmond.

She shook her head.

"Thank you; no. I feel better. I was very foolish; I was forgetting my years." She gave a wavering smile, and then seemed to regain the last of her self-control. "Please," she begged Jody, "go on with whatever you have to do. I'll sit here quietly."

"But I can't leave you and—"

"Please! It's just what I need. Please just go on as though I were not here."

She rose and took a few steps, and Jody saw that they

were firm ones. She left her and began to dish up the meal, and Desmond helped her.

There was silence until Estelle's voice was heard outside, and then Miss Bishop turned to Jody with eyes full of appeal.

"You won't say anything, will you?" she whispered.

"Of course I won't."

Estelle came in and sniffed the food-laden air.

"Lovely! I'm starving," she said. "Oh—Miss Bishop! That's where you've got to! The Professor's been looking for you."

"Where is he?" Miss Bishop's voice was almost her normal brisk one.

"He's in the study."

"I'll go to him. I've been getting in Jody's way, I'm afraid."

She went out, and the others went to the dining room. Michael was waiting for them, and Jody saw his eyes resting speculatively upon her and then moving to Desmond. She did not know what he was thinking, but she was able to guess the trend of his thoughts by the fact that he monopolized Desmond for the rest of the evening. He gave him little chance to talk to anybody else, took him off to his study to look at hunting prints after dinner, and when the moment came for the guest to leave, accompanied him to the door and saw him off.

"I like him," said Estelle, as he rejoined his wife and sister-in-law in the hall.

"Huntley?" he asked.

"Who else? I think he's terribly attractive."

"You do? So does somebody else," said Michael.

Jody ignored the challenge. Already halfway up the stairs, she threw him a smile and went on to her room.

Estelle came in later to say good night and to return a necklace she had borrowed.

"Miss Bishop had a sort of turn," Jody told her. "She played too much hide-and-seek with Fenella."

"You mean she felt ill?"

"Yes. Desmond and I found her leaning against a window in the hall, looking like death."

"Was that why she was sitting in the kitchen?"

"Yes. She asked me not to say anything to you then, so I didn't. But if you see Fenella trying to talk her into another hide-and-seek session, you might tactfully head her off."

"I will. Poor old Bishop. She won't like to feel she's past a romp." She yawned luxuriously and went to the door. "Tired?"

"No. Are you?"

"A bit. Michael was out today and I had three lots of parents to show round the school. I'm beginning to sound just like those guides who drag you round picture galleries; I just rattle it off and hope they're taking it in."

"Any probables?"

"Two, with luck. The third woman I think came just for the hell of it. She didn't listen to a word I said, she didn't look at a thing I pointed out, and then she went away and said she'd bring her husband. But I'm sorry Michael missed her."

"Why?"

"Because he would have enjoyed it. Good-looking, she was —and unusual. Very attractive—and a natural blonde. I had a good look, just to make sure, but it wasn't a bleached job. She was a natural-born blonde."

She was closing the door behind her before Jody spoke.

"What was her name?"

"The blonde?"

"Yes."

"She was a Mrs. Grierson," said Estelle, as she went out of the room.

### CHAPTER
# 13

FOR THE FIRST TIME in her life, Jody knew what it was to lie sleepless throughout the night. Tossing on her bed, hot and cold by turns, she longed for morning and its clear light.

Toward dawn, she slept fitfully, and woke at last heavy-eyed and with a mind that seemed to have stopped functioning. Nothing was connected. Nothing was clear, nothing real. Fear that she had thought stilled was plucking at her again, and she could summon no forces to fight it, for it was fear of the unknown.

Only one thought was clear: the need to see Desmond Huntley. She could not reason, but instinct reached out to one with whom she felt secure; someone who had moved forward with her to this place of fear, someone who would understand without the need for explanations.

She tried, when she got downstairs, to prepare breakfast in her usual cool and unhurried way, but her hands fumbled and she found it impossible to keep her mind on what she was doing.

She heard Estelle and Michael coming, and gripped the edge of the table in an effort to keep herself from trembling.

The woman called Laurie . . . here. The woman called Laurie coming here on the pretext of visiting the school. Laurie . . .

With an effort, she beat down her rising panic and managed to greet her sister and brother-in-law quietly when they entered the room.

"Fenella's still alseep," Estelle said. "Chasing Miss Bishop was obviously too much for both of them. Jody, you look tired."

"I am, a bit. I didn't sleep too well," said Jody.

She took Michael's warmed plate and walked over to put

his eggs and bacon on it, and heard his calm voice from behind her.

"Good weather ahead," he said. "We'll soon have Charles
back."

Charles!

The plate slipped from Jody's fingers and crashed in
pieces on the stone floor. Michael stooped to help her pick
them up, and his eyes, cool and searching, rested on her.

"The name rings a bell?" he inquired pleasantly.

"Michael, don't talk like that," said Estelle sharply.

He rose and place the broken pieces on the sink.

"I'm merely asking her if she remembers who Charles is,"
he said. "Any harm in that?"

"Here's your breakfast," said Jody.

"Thank you."

"And eat it without talking," directed Estelle.

"If you prefer it," said Michael politely. "But it would be
interesting to know why she looks distraught this morning
and why the mention of her fiancé's name costs us one of
our best breakfast plates."

Jody turned on him.

"If you want to know," she said, with a sort of desperate
calmness, "I'm worried. And I'm . . . I'm frightened."

His brows went up.

"Frightened?"

"Yes, frightened. Don't let it put you off your breakfast,
but there are things happening which . . . which you would
have known about if you'd shown any interest. There are
things—"

"—which you're longing to tell Charles?"

"I—"

She stopped and stared at him. There was a tense silence,
and then she spoke again in a calm voice.

"You're trying to say something," she told him.

"Nothing important. Just that in my opinion, which is
founded on observation, you haven't given Charles a serious
thought since you met this Huntley fellow. Isn't that true?"

"Look, Michael," began Estelle, "she—"

Michael's eyes had not left Jody.

"Isn't that true?" he repeated.

Jody's heart was thumping.

"You've no right—" she began—

"Isn't that true?"

She heard her own answer without realizing that she had spoken.

"Yes," she said. "It's true."

"Ah." Calmly he picked up his knife and fork and began to eat. "Just so long as you know."

"Why start something like this in the middle of breakfast?" asked Estelle angrily. "Why don't you ask her what's frightening her, and try to help her?"

"Because there's nothing to be frightened of." Michael buttered a piece of toast. "She has a simple choice: Vaughan or Huntley. If she thinks Charles will make a fuss, she's wrong. If I know him—and I know him better than anybody —he'll conclude that a girl who can't keep her mind on him for a few days while he's stuck across the Channel isn't the kind of girl to trust with his future."

"He wasn't stuck until the gale came up," pointed out Estelle heatedly. "He went over there because all he ever thinks of is his beastly sailing, and if he'd given more time to Jody and—"

"Please!" begged Jody.

She went to the door, and heard her sister's cry of dismay.

"You haven't eaten anything."

"I'm late." Jody went upstairs and, in a daze, got ready to leave. When she went downstairs, she found that Estelle had brought the car round.

"Get in," she said. "I'll take you to the station."

Thankfully, Jody climbed in, and Estelle drove for some minutes without speaking.

"Don't worry," she said at last. "Everything'll be all right."

Jody made no reply. Estelle stopped the car outside the little station, and looked at her anxiously as she got out.

"Don't let this frighten you," she said slowly. "Michael's right as far as that goes—there's nothing to be frightened of."

"I'm not. . . . It isn't that. . . ."

"Can't you tell me?" she said.

"Tonight," said Jody, "I'll tell you everything."

She reached the office and at once telephoned to Desmond Huntley.

"I've got to see you," she said. "It's . . . it's terribly important."

"Private or professional?" he asked.

"It's about Laurie. She came to the school."

"She . . . *what?*" His tone was incredulous.

"She came yesterday. Michael was out, and Estelle showed her over the school. She said she'd make an appointment and bring her husband and . . . Desmond, I'd like to talk about it, if you're free."

"Any time, any place."

"Somewhere quiet. Do you know that little road that runs off Revent Street between a big travel agent and a sort of fur shop?"

"I'll find it, but it would help if you could remember its name."

"I can't—but there's a little coffee bar halfway down it, and it's always quiet there in the evenings."

"Time?"

"I can't be there before six; I've got a late appointment today."

"Six o'clock, coffee bar in unknown road between unknown travel agent and unknown fur store. I'll be there."

And when Jody was making her way there, she saw Mr. Kennedy.

So remote was the chance which brought her, so unlikely the chance that made her choose this route, that when she saw him, her first thought was that she was imagining it all. But the stout form was only too real, and she passed to a fantastic conviction that Fate had led her to the spot. Only once before had she used this road; when she was taking a shortcut to a client's house. Then, she had paused to watch the building operations which had been in progress, turning some disused stables into the four tiny little mews cottages at which she was now staring.

It was a quiet, shadowed alley, little more than a court-yard, and the trim, expensive-looking little houses made a sharp contrast to the seedy buildings surrounding them. In the cobbled forecourt stood two or three cars—and a taxi. And out of the taxi was stepping Mr. Kennedy.

Jody did not know that she had moved, but she found herself on the opposite side of the road, her back toward the mews, facing a shabby shop whose window, empty and backed with dirty brown paper, served as a mirror and gave her a view of Mr. Kennedy's actions.

He did not, as she expected, pay off the taxi and go into one of the houses, and disappointment swept through her, for in one of them, she had felt certain, would have been Laurie, waiting for him. But having got out of the taxi,

Mr. Kennedy made no move toward the houses; instead, he said a word to the driver, lit a cigarette, offered one to the man and then began to pace slowly to and fro. He was meeting somebody, and he had arrived at the rendezvous first.

Jody turned, and with deliberate steps crossed the street and walked into the courtyard. She had to follow Mr. Kennedy a little way, for his pacing was taking him away from her. She came up behind him and spoke his name.

"Mr. Kennedy."

He swung round. The movement was swift, almost catlike, and she knew that she had taken him unawares—but there was not more than a flicker of expression in his eyes before they became the hard little black stones she remembered.

"Miss Hern!" He gave her a slight bow, and smiled. "This is a very pleasant surprise."

"Did you visit somebody at the school the other night?" Jody asked him.

Her directness seemed, for a moment, to nonplus him; he gave a swift glance in the direction of the driver, and then assured himself that the man was out of hearing; then he spoke without answering her question.

"Are you visiting somebody here?"

"No. I just happened to pass, and I saw you."

"Then perhaps I can give you a lift to wherever you were going? I have a taxi here."

"Aren't you waiting for somebody?"

He glanced at his watch, and shrugged.

"It is late; I shall not wait any longer. Shall we go?"

"I'd like to talk to you, please," said Jody.

He gave her a brief, measuring glance, and something in her bearing seemed to decide him.

"We shall talk—but not here," he said. He took her arm and led her to the taxi, gave a direction and handed her in. "We shall talk over a drink."

"Where are we going?" she asked.

He laughed—an unexpectedly loud, jovial laugh. Still smiling, he turned to her.

"You have cast me as a villain, I think. But if I wanted to carry off young ladies, perhaps I would be wiser to use my own car and not a London taxi. I am not taking you to a disused warehouse in the purlieus; we are merely going to the Merlin."

A few minutes later, they were seated upon two stools at the bar.

"It was there"—Jody nodded toward the doors—"that Mrs. Grierson came in."

"And I came in a car and I took her away—and you saw me." His manner had become almost fatherly. Jody sensed that he had summed up the situation and decided that he had it well in hand.

"Did you send me that anonymous letter asking me to come here some time ago?" she asked.

He took his drink from a waiter, and poured Jody's coffee out of its tiny plated pot.

"Did you?" she asked again.

"There were two letters, were there not?" he asked.

"If you know that, you must have written them."

"Not necessarily." His black eyes rested speculatively upon her. "Have you become a detective?"

"I didn't want to. When you pretended to be the Reception Manager and came out to talk about Mrs. Grierson, I hadn't the least desire to get mixed up in anything to do with her . . . or with you. But there's a point beyond which it's just silly to . . . to ignore signs."

"And there's a point," said Mr. Kennedy silkily, "beyond which it's just silly not to."

"I don't understand you."

"In deciding not to be what you call silly, couldn't you become foolhardy?"

"If you didn't want me to become interested, why did you go to so much trouble to get me interested in the first place?"

Mr. Kennedy's short, fat fingers fiddled absently with the stem of his glass. She knew he was thinking hard, and she waited until he looked up.

"Well?" she asked.

He spoke slowly and soberly.

"I will be frank with you, Miss Hern. When I went out and spoke to you—spoke to you and to Commander Huntley —I did it because I did not know either of you. If I had known who you were, what you both were, I would have let you drive away and I would have said nothing."

"But you did say something, and you did, as far as I can make out, send those anonymous letters, and you did go down to the school. Nobody wants to get themselves mixed up in matters which don't concern them. But on the other hand, nobody can look on indefinitely while people make sinister moves all round them. Especially when the moves involve friends and relations."

"You are referring to Commander Huntley?"

"No, I'm not. I'm referring to my aunt, Lady Cleeve. You don't look like a house-breaker, Mr. Kennedy, but somebody entered her house in Knightsbridge and—"

"But nothing was stolen," Mr. Kennedy stated calmly.

She stared at him, anger rising slowly and showing in her cheeks.

"Then it was you?"

"I—and others." He twisted himself round to face her, and spoke abruptly. "Look, Miss Hern, I will tell you why I acted as I did—and then your mind will be set at rest. You are worried, you are perhaps alarmed—but you need not be. I am sorry, more sorry than I can say that I drew you into any matter concerning Mrs. Grierson, for Mrs. Grierson is not a person with whom I would ever wish you to become entangled."

"But you were only too anxious, that first day outside Dorset Court, that we should—"

"Wait, please. I will try to explain." The black eyes held her own. "First: it was necessary for me to find Laurie."

"Mrs. Grierson?"

"She is not Mrs. Grierson, but that does not matter to you. I had to find her. She had left Dorset Court—for Kenya, she said, but I thought it likely that she would be somewhere in London. She left no clues—"

"Except blood on the drawing-room carpet."

"That was not a clue. I was at Dorset Court, inquiring for her—and I learned that two young people had also been making inquiries. Now: I had not seen you, either of you; I did not know who you were, but people who inquire for the Lauries of this world do so for one of two reasons: because they are her friends and wish to find her . . . or because they are not her friends and wish to find her. I had nothing, then, to go upon—but you, I thought, might know something, something that would lead you to Laurie. And if you, then why not myself too? So I went out and spoke to you— and then I . . . I kept you, as you might say, in sight. And made certain investigations in order to assure myself that in spite of your saying you did not know Laurie, you had had no previous connection with her."

"And so you removed all those papers about me from my aunt's house?"

"Yes. They will be returned to her soon, and she will perhaps forgive me for having done what I did. But it was necessary, because you see . . . I had to find Laurie."

"But when you came here, here to the Merlin—"

"I had already located Laurie. But I still could not be certain whether you and the Commander knew her or not. And so I . . . may I say lured you both to this place, and I asked certain of my friends to keep close to you both and to observe you with keen attention when Laurie came in. She came in—and it was quite clear that neither of you had ever seen her before. And so I regretted my action, and I resolved that in future, my dealings with Laurie would not involve you."

"But your visit to the school—was that connected with Laurie?"

He smiled.

"The one place I would not look for Laurie," he said, "would be in Sussex."

"But she was there. She was at the school yesterday," said Jody.

Instantly, she regretted the words. For Mr. Kennedy, one moment casual, smooth, paternal, had the next instant frozen into immobility and was staring at her out of eyes that had suddenly become terrifying. Round her were scores of people, gay, chattering—and yet Jody felt cold fear filling her heart.

She heard, it seemed from a distance, Mr. Kennedy's grating statement.

"You are mistaken."

She forced herself to go on meeting his gaze.

"I'm not mistaken. When I got home last night, my sister told me that one of the parents she had taken over the school was a Mrs. Grierson."

"You are certainly mistaken. Laurie is not Mrs. Grierson, and she had no children."

"My sister described her, as you described her to me. I'm quite certain she was Laurie."

Mr. Kennedy sat for one moment more in the curiously

still pose. Then he had plunged his hand in his pocket and was bringing out some loose money and signaling a waiter.

"You will forgive me," he said quietly to Jody, "for my impoliteness—but I have remembered an important appointment. Perhaps you will allow me to drop you wherever you wish to go?"

Lying, like everything else, Jody found, improved with practice.

"I'm going to see Lady Cleeve," she said. "If you wouldn't mind calling a taxi for me—"

"But of course."

He put her into a taxi and himself gave Lady Cleeve's address; then he had bowed and she was being driven away without any knowledge of why the mention of Laurie's visit to the school should have brought to an abrupt termination her talk with Mr. Kennedy. He had given her no further opportunity for question or argument; she had been ushered out of the Merlin and into the taxi in the space of a few seconds.

She leaned forward and spoke to the driver—and then the taxi had turned and was taking her speedily, not to say dangerously, to the coffee bar at which she had arranged to meet Desmond Huntley.

He was waiting at the door. She flung herself out, gave the driver the money she held ready in hand, and turned to see Desmond's anxious eyes upon her.

"I'm late; I'm sorry," she brought out breathlessly. "I couldn't help it but . . . we've got to hurry. Where's your car?"

"Just there." He was leading her to it, putting her in without words and hurrying round to take his place at the wheel.

"Where?" he asked.

"I'll direct you. Can you drive as fast as possible?"

"If you'll give me sensible directions. What's the hurry?"

She told him, her account interspersed with brief, clear orders as to the direction he was to take. The car edged round corners, roared up empty side streets and snaked in and out of the traffic on main roads. By the time they had drawn near to the mews at which she had seen Mr. Kennedy, Desmond was in command of the situation.

"You think he'll go back?"

"I'm sure he will. He was waiting to meet somebody."

"That's a long time ago."

"No, it isn't. We weren't long at the Merlin—and we ought to have a start, because he had to wait for another taxi after I'd left. Why are you stopping?"

"Because we can't drive up and let him see us."

"But—"

"We've got to find a place from which we can see without being seen. Come on."

He stopped the car in a street that ran at right angles to the mews, and got out and looked about him. Opposite was a shabby building used as offices; these were closed for the night, but the main entrance—a door with brown paint peeling off it—stood open. Into this Desmond led Jody. They fumbled their way up the first few stairs with no light except that which came from the door; then they reached a landing and an unscreened window above gave them not only enough light to take the last stairs at a rush, but also offered them a good view of the courtyard opposite.

The cars were still there—but no taxi. Jody waited a few minutes to get her breath, and fought off the thought that Mr. Kennedy might, after all, not return.

"He'll come," said Desmond, in answer to her look.

"How do you know?"

"There doesn't seem to be anybody waiting for him, so perhaps they got tired and left—but I think Kennedy'll come back on the off-chance of catching them. Remember that he had no opportunity of telling them that he wouldn't be here; as he didn't send a message, they ought to assume that he'll turn up."

"But if—"

"And here he comes," said Desmond.

Jody stared down at the little courtyard. Mr. Kennedy was stepping out of a taxi; Mr. Kennedy, with his black, expressionless eyes and his certainty that Laurie could not have been at the school . . .

For a moment he stood looking this way and that. He turned, and Jody felt Desmond jerk her back from the window.

"Nobody's there to meet him," she said, and found that she had whispered the words.

"Wait," said Desmond. "He's just making sure that you're not around again, that's all."

They looked down cautiously. Mr. Kennedy had walked to

the house at the end of the row and given a sign. From the small archway that led to the side door, Jody saw a man emerge and walk forward to join him.

It was her brother-in-law, Michael Page.

CHAPTER

14

IT SEEMED A LONG TIME before Jody heard Desmond's voice.

"You're trembling," he said.

He was standing behind her, and she did not turn. She felt his hands on her shoulders, steadying her, and she was grateful, for once again they were watching, as they had watched before, Mr. Kennedy driving away with someone they had recognized, leaving them puzzled and helpless.

"We . . . we shouldn't have come up," said Jody at last, in a voice she tried in vain to keep steady. "We should have stayed down there, and then we could have . . . we could have spoken to them. We . . ."

"I'm glad we didn't."

She turned at last, and at the sight of her face, white and strained, he took her hand in his and led her to the stairs.

"Come on," he said.

She said nothing; she allowed him to lead her to the place at which he had left his car. He put her in and stood looking at her anxiously.

"There's no reason to look like that," he said gently, after a time. "Your brother-in-law was probably the next on the list for an anonymous letter from our friend Kennedy."

"No." There was certainty in Jody's voice. "Michael wouldn't have taken any notice of an anonymous letter. He would have torn it up—just as we would have done if we hadn't . . . if we hadn't been . . . been caught up with Mr. Kennedy."

"How do you know Michael isn't? He kept an appointment with him in a rather seedy part of town, and—"

"Could it have been . . . because of me?"

He came round and sat beside her and turned her face toward his.

"So that's it? You're worrying yourself sick because you think you've got your brother-in-law into something?"

144

"No. I'm frightened, that's all."

"I'd rather see your brother-in-law dealing with Kennedy than watch you trying to do it. I don't know Michael well, but I don't feel he's a man I'd like to talk into doing anything he didn't want to do."

"You saw him just now. Did he look like a man who was doing something he wanted to do? Did he look like—" She stopped and put out a hand gropingly and he took it firmly into his own. "Desmond, I'm frightened."

"I can see you are," he said gently. "But aren't you reading too much into this?"

"You and I agreed to try to find out what it was that I'd got involved in. Now I find that it involves another member of my family. What do I do? Go home and wait for Michael to explain what he was doing with Kennedy? Go home and say nothing to Estelle? Go home and sit about waiting for somebody to come and straighten out—"

"Wait." His calm voice stopped her. "We're not proving very clever as investigators, but one thing we can do: proceed to make what we can of the evidence. We've just seen your brother-in-law keeping a rather shady appointment— shady because the place was obviously chosen to avoid running into anybody he was likely to know. Kennedy had something to say, and he summoned your brother-in-law, perhaps by using your name. But this doesn't mean that Michael's involved. Kennedy says what he has to say, and your brother-in-law probably has to decide whether to keep it to himself, or to tell you. You'll know when you go home to-night. I'll drive you down, and if you'll let me, I'll stay with you while you ask him what he was doing with Kennedy."

He waited for her answer, but Jody was staring down unseeingly at the hand that was clasping her own. Then her eyes went to Desmond, and he was shocked at the expression in them.

"What is it?" she asked slowly. "Oh Desmond, what is it? How could I have got caught up in something like this? In all my life, I—"

"What are you frightened of?" he broke in to ask.

She stared at him uncomprehendingly.

"What am I . . ."

"I'm trying to find out what's making you look like this. I don't think you're frightened for your own safety—or are you? It wouldn't be a reflection on your courage if you were.

There are some things that every right-minded citizen ought to be frightened of, and I wouldn't blame you for expecting a pair of hands to emerge from the blackness and fasten themselves round your throat. But—"

"It isn't that. Anything definite would be . . . would be almost a relief. It's this . . . this sitting about having inexplicable things happening and not being able to understand, not being able to do anything. I . . . I feel suffocated. I feel as though I'm feeling my way about in a pitch-black room, and keep touching something . . . something horrible. And there's something else. There's still . . . deep down . . . that fear I had when I tried to understand what had happened to me that morning. It was there before I ever saw Kennedy, before I ever set eyes on Laurie. It went away for a little while—and now it's back again."

"You mean that you think something did happen to make you lose consciousness—something apart from falling down those stairs?"

"Yes. Do you still think it was only an accident?"

"I never did think it was only an accident," he reminded her.

"And Kennedy knows what happened, and he's—"

"I don't think he knows. He's not acting like a man who knows. He's acting like a man who wants to know. If he knew, he'd act; I'm sure of that. He's like us—he's groping for something."

"Or someone."

"Or someone. And the only ray of light I see in this blackout is that you're not the someone. Why? Because everybody knows where to find you. Kennedy knows. Laurie knows. And whatever it was you got involved in, they know you can't remember anything about it—and they're concerned, now, in keeping you out of the picture. And that suits me. If I thought you were in danger yourself, I'd . . ."

"You'd what?"

"I'd go to the police."

"How could you go to the police if Michael's involved in it?"

"That"—he spoke decisively—"we can find out. All we do is drive down to Broome and ask him for a straight answer to a straight question: what he was doing in Kennedy's company. But first, we'll go somewhere and I'll put a good, strong drink into you."

"No. No, thank you. I . . . I don't feel like walking into any public place. I . . . I've got an awful feeling I might howl at any moment."

"Then howl." He released her hand, got out a large square of handkerchief and shook open its folds. "Here. Cry, and you'll feel a good deal better."

Jody shook her head and spoke tremulously.

"No. What I'd like is to . . . to go along to Aunt Essie's and have some strong coffee."

"If I take you there, she'll freeze me out."

"It won't be for long."

"I hope not. If you've any charitable feelings, you'll get me out of there—fast."

He was glad to see her smile. He drove to the house and they went up the steps and Jody pressed the bell.

It was Lady Cleeve who answered the door, and something in her white, strained look made Jody reach out and take her hands in a firm grasp.

"Aunt Essie—what's the matter?" She moved her aunt gently aside, came in with Desmond and signaled to him to close the door behind them. "What's happened, Aunt Essie?"

"Nothing," Lady Cleeve's voice was quiet, but it was clear that she was struggling for self-control. "Nothing has happened."

Jody led the way into the drawing room. Desmond drew forward a chair and settled Lady Cleeve in it and then brought her a drink.

"That's better," he said, when she had taken some of it.

Jody was on her knees beside her aunt, the long white hands clasped in her own brown ones.

"Have you had bad news?" she asked.

"No."

"Something's happened to upset you badly. Can't you tell me what it is? Shall I send Desmond away and—"

"No. I shall be all right in a few moments. I—"

She paused. Jody was rising slowly to her feet, her eyes on a large, open envelope that lay on the table beside her aunt, some papers half out of it. She picked it up and held it, with the papers, in her hand.

"These . . . came back?" she asked slowly.

"Yes."

"And the envelope isn't stamped. So they came . . . they were brought by somebody."

"Yes."

"Kennedy?" asked Desmond.

"Yes," said Lady Cleeve.

"When?"

"He left"—she glanced at the clock—"eight minutes ago. When you rang the bell, I thought . . . I wondered if he had come back."

"Why did he frighten you?" asked Desmond. "Did he threaten you?"

"Threaten? No."

Lady Cleeve's manner was returning to normal, and Desmond watched her with some of his dislike turning to admiration. She had obviously had a shock, and a bad one, but she had fought a battle with panic—and won. She was still white, still shaken, but she had herself perfectly well in hand.

"He brought back these papers—and said something to frighten you," said Jody.

"Yes." Lady Cleeve's eyes rested quietly upon her. "He told me something that frightened me."

"What was it, Aunt Essie?"

"He told me that you are in danger."

There was a long, breathless silence. It was broken by Lady Cleeve's deliberately quiet voice.

"He asked me to take you away for a time."

"If he asked you that," said Desmond, "he must have given you a reason."

"He brought the papers and returned them to me with apologies. He told me that Jody is in danger—grave danger —and that I must take her abroad with me for a little while. That was all."

"Not quite all," said Jody. "He must have explained who he was. He must have told you how he came to have these papers. He must have—"

"He rang the bell. Clarice was out, and I went to the door. I had no idea who he was. He bowed and asked if he might come in and speak to me for a few—a very few minutes; he had some papers to return to me. I asked him to come in."

"But if you knew he had the papers, you must have known that he was the man who had broken into the house to get them—and you asked him in!" said Jody.

"I had to hear what he had to say. He apologized for having taken the papers—and then he told me what I've just told you. And then he went away." She turned suddenly and spoke in a voice very different from the calm, cold one she had been using. "Jody, you will come, won't you?"

"No," said Jody.

Lady Cleeve stared at her, and seemed about to speak, when Desmond interrupted.

"If you'll listen to good advice, Jody," he said, "you'll go away with your aunt."

"I won't go away," said Jody steadily. "I've never hurt anybody and I don't believe anybody wants to hurt me. You've just been saying so yourself—you said that if anybody had wanted to hurt me, they knew where I was, and they could have—"

"Mr. Kennedy," broke in Lady Cleeve, "told me that he had had a meeting with Michael."

"Did he tell you why?"

"Yes. He said that he telephoned to Michael this morning and asked him to come to London and meet him. When they met, he told him that Jody was in danger and should be removed for a time—taken away, taken abroad. Michael sent him to me. He explained that he himself had no influence with Jody and that there was only one person who could persuade her: myself. That is why Mr. Kennedy came here."

"Didn't he tell you anything about the kind of danger I was in?" asked Jody.

"Nothing. But he said it in a way that made me believe him."

"Well, I don't believe him," said Jody.

"I do," said Desmond. "Kennedy, in my opinion, is a man who wouldn't go to all this trouble to frighten your aunt unless he had a good reason for it."

"The only reason he wants me out of the way," said Jody, "is because I've begun to frighten him. I don't know how, but I've got in his way. And he doesn't want me in his way."

"And doesn't that put you in danger?" asked Desmond.

Jody faced them both.

"Please listen to me," she said quietly. "I've done nothing whatsoever to get myself caught up with crooks like Mr. Kennedy—but I've learned something lately, and that is that however frightened you are, fear isn't any worse than . . . than this ghastly uncertainty. I don't want anything to happen to me. I'm just as anxious as anybody else to stay out of harm's way. But if I go away with Aunt Essie, I shall go quite slowly and quite quietly crazy. I shall go out of my mind. I shall wake up in the night screaming—and all the screams will be questions. Who is Mr. Kennedy, and why? Who is Laurie, and why? Who—and why? Why—and who?"

"You've made your point," said Desmond. "You won't go away, and that's crazy too. And now I'm going to take you home and we're going to talk to your brother-in-law."

"Why?" asked Lady Cleeve.

"Because we saw him meet Kennedy less than an hour ago," said Desmond, "and—"

"You saw him?"

"Yes. Did Kennedy tell you he'd run into Jody—unwillingly?"

"Yes. She told him that she was coming to see me, but he was not sure whether she was telling the truth or not. So before coming here himself, he fetched the papers. He said that if Jody had been here, he would have used them as an excuse for coming to see me, and then he would have gone away and come back later."

"I let him direct the taxi to your house," said Jody, "and then I went to the place where Desmond and I had arranged to meet, and we got back to Mr. Kennedy's meeting place in time to see Michael with him. There was no time to talk to them; they got into the taxi that was waiting, and drove away. And after that, Kennedy brought you the papers. Since I ran into him this evening, he's done some thinking and he feels that I've got more curiosity than sense and—"

"And so you have," said Desmond.

"Maybe—but what I'm concerned with at this moment isn't my safety, but my sanity. I'm sorry Mr. Kennedy has dragged Michael into this, and I'm sorry Aunt Essie's had her house ransacked, but I'm not going to be shipped over to Italy or Greece in order to oblige Mr. Kennedy. Aunt Essie, didn't you ask him why he took those papers?"

"Of course. He said that it was to assure himself that you had no connection, now or in the past, knowingly or unknowingly, with a woman he called Laurie. Jody . . . please, please come away with me."

Jody sat on the arm of her aunt's chair and took her hand.

"Darling Aunt Essie," she said gently, "I love you and I'm grateful to you—but if people want to interfere in other people's lives, as Mr. Kennedy is trying to do in mine, they ought to have good reasons to give. I don't like Mr. Kennedy, and I don't trust him and I'm absolutely certain that if he orders me out of the country, it isn't for my health, but for his own."

"Look—" began Desmond, and was halted by Lady Cleeve.

"It's no use," she said quickly. "I know my niece, and you don't. There's nothing more to be said."

They drove home in silence, and Jody leaned back and gave herself up to the feeling of moving swiftly, silently toward—what?

She didn't know—but seated beside Desmond, his large, strong body close to her own, she knew that she was traveling, at last, without fear. The struggle, for her, was over. She knew at last that her state of mind during the past few days had been caused only partly by the inexplicable events that had followed her accident. Beyond, below, there had been the knowledge that she had come to a turning point in her life. The old, the familiar, had sufficed—and now it sufficed no longer. Michael's words this morning had brought the conflict into the open, and at the same time had resolved it. She did not know what the future held; she knew only that her mind, at last, was clear.

She heard Desmond's voice.

"Good weather," he pointed out. "That means that Charles will be back."

"He's on his way. He's due tomorrow morning."

There was a pause.

"I'm sorry," said Desmond at last.

She made no reply. After a brief silence, he began to speak in a slow, almost absent tone.

"I'm sorry," he said, "because from the very first, I had a feeling—about you and me. Perhaps when a girl begins by falling into your arms, you begin at the wrong end . . . but it wasn't only that. It was a feeling that you and I . . . fitted. There were no preliminaries, and no need for any. From the first, I seemed to find it impossible to look at what surrounded you—family, fiancé—because I could only see you. It seemed to me that Heaven had lifted you up, out of your frame, and put you into my arms. It seemed right and natural. From the first, I tried to keep your fiancé in my mind—but my heart never really believed that he was there. There just seemed you—and me. I didn't even, if you can believe me, have to ask myself if I was in love with you. I just was; finish. Nobody seemed to have any real connection with us—perhaps because Betsy had linked us together and given us a tie that shut everyone else out. I loved you, and I didn't even worry about the fact that things couldn't go on for long as they were. The world had to come back. Charles had to come back. But I'm sorry."

There was a long silence.

"So am I," said Jody quietly at last.

For a moment, she thought that he had not heard. Then she found the car drawing to the side of the road, drawing off the road and coming to a halt. He switched off the engine and turned to look at her.

"Say that again," he said slowly.

"I said I'm sorry."

"Sorry that . . . that Charles is coming back?"

"Yes."

"You mean . . . you mean you . . ."

"Yes," said Jody.

He sat without moving for a few moments, and then he drew a long, difficult breath.

"You know what you're saying?"

"Yes." She gave a tremulous laugh. "I'm only thankful that you . . . that you said it first."

"You're engaged to another man—remember?"

"Yes. And all I feel is a terrible sense of guilt—at having worn a ring that should have meant so much, and didn't mean anything."

"When did you know?"

"That I didn't love Charles? I acknowledged it, openly and audibly, at a quarter past eight this morning. But what you just said . . . that goes for me, too. From the first, everything seemed right."

He put a hand under her chin and raised her face until he looked into her eyes.

"I said I loved you," he told her slowly. "Do you know what I meant? Do you understand how I feel? Do you know that every moment of the day, I think about you? Do you know that I go to sleep at night with you in my mind, and wake up in the morning remembering you, what you look like, what you sound like? Do you know what I've been longing to do?"

He put his arms round her and drew her close. His lips

came down on hers, and stayed there, warm and firm and seeking. He kissed her mouth, her eyes; his lips strayed round her face, and came to rest once more upon her mouth. She closed her eyes and let peace and warmth steal over her, and then her arms went up and clasped themselves round his neck, to draw him closer.

"Jody," he whispered. "Are you sure . . . quite, quite sure?"

"Quite sure," she said.

They drew away from one another and tried to pierce the soft dusk and see one another's faces.

"I . . . I love you," he said slowly. "I love you so much, Jody. I hate the feeling that I've taken you away from another man, but—"

"There was never anything like this," she said, "between Charles and myself."

"He might have felt it without being able to show it."

"He might have felt it. But I didn't," said Jody.

"You said you acknowledged it openly and audibly."

"Yes. To Michael and Estelle, this morning. So telling them won't be hard. Telling Charles . . . that won't be easy."

"Shouldn't I be there when you talk to him?"

"No. Desmond—"

"Well?"

"Before . . . before this happened, did you believe people could fall in love at first sight?"

"Yes. Nancy and her husband did. They met at Victoria Station; they'd both been to see friends off and they both arrived just as the train left. They stood there looking after it and she said Damn and he said Blast and they looked at one another—and haven't looked at anybody else since. And neither of them even felt at all surprised; it happened, and they never had any doubts—then or now. Nancy says that falling in love is like shopping—you look at a lot of things and can't make up your mind, and suddenly . . . there's exactly what you want, exactly what you've been looking for. And if you're wise, you grab it and stop looking. In your case, you thought you saw what you wanted—but you were wrong. And I'm sorry for Charles. I'm damned sorry for Charles . . ."

Jody said nothing. She had never, she thought, taken first place in Charles's plans for the future. He loved her, but she did not think that he would be lost without her. There were other things he wanted as much—more. And for herself . . . she knew that she had never loved—until now. She had drifted, in that old life, without questioning, without probing. And then she had fallen down a flight of stairs—and her life was changed forever.

She lay unresisting in Desmond's arms, happier than she had ever imagined she could be, and filled with wonder at the thought that she could have lived so long imagining herself in love with Charles. Nothing, she knew, would ever take from her the sweetness of this moment. She had touched Heaven, and one part of her would remain up there in gratitude.

It was almost midnight when they reached the house. Desmond walked with her to the front door and stood looking down at her.

"Jody—won't you think over what your aunt said?"

"I'm not going away, Desmond. I'm not frightened of Mr. Kennedy."

"If he says you're in danger—"

"I don't believe it. At least"—she corrected herself—"I don't believe him. I'm staying where I am."

He said nothing more. She stood watching him as he drove away, and then she turned and went slowly into the house, closing the front door behind her and drawing the heavy bolts.

She turned and went slowly toward the staircase, her mind full of love and thankfulness. Desmond . . . large, awkward, strong, gentle . . .

She heard a cautious knock, and turned with a smile. He had forgotten to say something—or he had returned to feel her close to him once more, as she longed to feel him.

She walked to the door and drew back the bolts and opened it, the smile still on her lips.

On the threshold stood the woman called Laurie.

# CHAPTER

## 15

LAURIE WAS THE FIRST to speak.

"You know who I am?"

Jody looked at her, and the look was a calm one, for there was nothing in her mind but a conviction that this was not, could not be happening. She was not standing here at midnight in conversation with a beautiful blonde who—last touch of the fantastic—spoke with a foreign accent. This was going beyond the realm of hard fact into the land of too-fancy. This was . . . this was a bad dream.

Laurie's words, however, sounded factual enough as she answered her own question.

"Yes, you know me. Our friend Mr. Kennedy has spoken to you about me?"

Jody did not reply for a moment. She was studying the woman standing before her, and finding her as beautiful as on the evening she had seen her at the Merlin Bar. The light from the hall shone on her, making her look younger, less hard than she had looked that evening. Her skin, Jody saw, was like her hair—natural, untouched and of silken beauty.

"We can't talk here," she said quietly. "Won't you—"

"No. If he told you that I am Mrs. Grierson, that was a lie."

Jody met the hard blue glance.

"But you were in Dorset Court that morning?"

"When you had your . . . accident? Yes, I was there."

"And I went to your apartment—by mistake?"

Laurie gave a slow, amused smile.

"Certainly it was a mistake," she agreed. "People should not make mistakes of that kind."

"What happened that morning, Mrs. Grierson. Please— please tell me!"

"I have told you that I am not Mrs. Grierson."

"You were called Mrs. Grierson—and you vanished the same morning and nobody knew where you had gone."

"Nobody at Dorset Court," corrected Laurie coolly.

Jody stepped back and opened the door wide.

"Please come inside and talk," she begged. "There's so much—"

"—you want to know? That I believe. But I am not coming in. I have only to come to say something to you."

"What is it?"

Laurie's expression did not seem to change, but the eyes into which Jody was looking became suddenly blank and expressionless.

"You must go away—at once," she said.

Her voice was quiet, but it held such deadly menace that Jody's hands crept up her arms until she seemed to be hugging herself in a curious attitude of protection.

"If you tell me why—" she began hesitatingly.

"I will tell you nothing—except to go. Shall I tell you what will happen if you do not go?"

"Mr. Kennedy"—Jody stopped and cleared her throat—"Mr. Kennedy has already—"

"—warned you. He is a fool. When you wish people to do something, you do not waste time trying to frighten them; in one sentence, you tell them what to expect. I heard you say just now, to that man, that you were not afraid. For yourself, perhaps not. For your little niece—the little one who is called Fenella—I think you would think again."

There was a short, deadly silence, out of which Jody heard her own voice.

"Y—you're not frightening me," she said.

"You don't believe I could hurt the child?"

Jody stared at her.

"Yes. Yes, I believe you could," she said slowly. "You could hurt anybody if it suited you. You're . . ."

"A woman with a purpose," said Laurie. "Will you go away?"

"If I say I will, why can't you tell me what happened that morning? Nothing that happened was my fault. The whole thing was a mistake. I'd never heard of you. I didn't mean to go to Number Four. But I did go there—and you were there."

"Yes, I was there."

"And there was blood on the carpet."

"Who . . . ah, Mr. Kennedy again. Yes, there was blood. Not much blood."

"But it was . . . it was mine?"

"It was yours. It was necessary to hurt you a little—not much. You were better again in a day or two."

"What happened? What happened to me?" Jody's voice was urgent. "Nothing's worse than not knowing . . . nothing."

Laurie studied her curiously.

"You really want to know?"

"I'd give anything to know."

"Then perhaps"—Laurie for the first time seemed to hesitate—"then I do not see why I should not tell you."

"Will you come inside and tell me?"

"No. It will not take long. And then—you will go away?"

"If it means keeping harm from Fenella, I'll go anywhere."

"Very well. Then I shall tell you what happened to you on that morning. It will not take long. You came to the building. You were seen; you were recognized."

"By whom?"

"Wait. You were obviously going to give one of your beauty treatments. . . . There was nothing to worry about; you would go to an apartment; any apartment but mine. But . . . it began to look as though you were not going to any other apartment. You looked at the board with the names. You looked at your notebook; you looked again, and you seemed to be looking straight at Number Four. You turned. Somebody was getting into one of the elevators, and he waited for you. But the lift was crowded, and you drew back and said 'Thank you—it's only on the first floor.' And you went toward the staircase. Not the main staircase; not to the small staircase which led to other apartments on the first floor. The staircase you used would lead you to one apartment only: mine."

"And I went to your apartment, and rang the bell—"

"No. You did not get as far as my apartment. You met somebody on the way. You did not see him. You had stopped to look out of the window in the corridor, and so he was able to come up behind you. He used you gently. He—"

"Who? Who?" broke in Jody. "I'd never hurt anybody—why should anybody want to hurt me?"

"There were. . . reasons," said Laurie.

"Somebody hit me—is that it?"

"That is it."

"Who? Who was it?"

"I said that I would tell you, and I will." Laurie's voice was mocking. "You will be—"

There was a sharp, cracking noise and the words became a low gurgling sound. Jody, numb with terror, saw the woman standing in front of her sway, put out groping hands and then fall in a heap at her feet.

Staring down at her, Jody could hear sounds—screams, loud and repeated, and footsteps, and then voices. From upstairs came Estelle. From the garage came Michael, running swiftly. From the cottages came the Major, stumbling in his haste; behind him, the Professor, groping blindly without his glasses and fumbling with the cord of his dressing gown; Miss Bishop, still fully dressed. They came and stood round Jody, but the screams went on and on—and then Michael raised a hand and Jody felt the sting of it as it struck hard at her cheek, and the screaming stopped abruptly and she realized that it had been coming from herself.

She felt Estelle's arms round her, and saw Michael stooping to look at the woman lying at their feet. Then he straightened and looked slowly round the circle of faces: the Major, his mouth hanging open, his eyes horror-stricken; Miss Bishop, trembling violently, the Professor, peering sightlessly from one to the other and still breathing fast from the unaccustomed speed with which he had come across the lawn. It was he who spoke first.

"Is she . . ."

He paused, and Michael answered the unspoken question. "She's dead."

The Professor spoke slowly.

"Then it was a shot. I was asleep, but . . . I have awakened before to that sound. I could not mistake it." He pressed his hands together in a curious, kneading gesture, and looked at Michael. "She was leaving the house?"

"No." Michael glanced at Jody. "No. She was with Jody . . . I think."

"Yes," said Jody.

Miss Bishop spoke in a dazed voice.

"Hadn't she better be . . . be carried inside?"

"Nobody must touch her." Michael's voice was calm. "The police will have to see her just as she is." He was at the telephone, dialing, and they waited in silence as the words, incredible in the quiet, dim hall, were spoken: accident, fatal; woman shot dead; shot through the back . . .

Estelle's eyes, wide and unbelieving, rested on her husband as he put down the receiver.

"Murder," she breathed. "Oh, Michael . . ."

"It's all right." He spoke steadily, but his face was ghastly. "It's all right. The police will be here in a little while."

He walked across the hall and put on more lights, and the company, unfamiliar, disheveled-looking, were clearly revealed.

"My spectacles," said the Professor. "I must get them. I see nothing."

"Don't be long," said Michael.

The Professor looked dismayed.

"I must come back?" he asked.

"I think so. The police will want to question everybody."

"They will not come to the cottage to ask me questions?"

"I think they'd prefer to see everybody here."

"I will not be long," said the Professor.

Nobody spoke during his absence. As he come up the steps once more, the headlights of a car pierced the darkness outside. A moment later, a car had stopped and three men were getting out of it.

The next few hours passed, for Jody, in a dream. Once she went upstairs and went into Fenella's bedroom; the small figure lay with arms outflung, deeply, peacefully asleep. Jody stood looking down at the flushed face, and she remembered the woman called Laurie, and the words she had uttered, words that threatened danger to a child. Laurie . . . now lying dead on the cold steps, with her white skin and her fair silken hair and her red blood creeping from under her body . . .

Down in the hall, the police asked questions and noted down the answers. Jody told her story. Desmond Huntley had brought her home, had left. She had locked the door—and had heard a knock. She had opened the door. She tried to recall the words Laurie had spoken, and her own replies. She had been on the verge of learning something—but Laurie had died with a name on her lips, killed by a bullet that came out of the dark.

Michael had been in London, he said. He had returned late. He had put away his car, and had closed the doors of the garage and was in the act of walking toward the house when he heard the shot, and came round the corner of the house to see a woman falling. . . .

Miss Bishop had not been in bed; she had been reading and she had gone into the kitchen to make herself a hot drink. She had been pouring it out when she heard the shot; she had dropped the saucepan and broken the cup—and come running.

The Major had not been in bed, but he had fallen asleep in his chair. He had been awakened, he said, not by the shot but by the sound of the Professor running out of his house. He had followed him, and they had heard Miss Bishop coming out of her cottage and calling to them, but they had not waited to answer her. The Professor could only repeat that the shot had awakened him.

At about half-past four, Jody went into the kitchen to make some coffee. Her movements were mechanical. She stood trying to remember how many cups she should make, found her brain refusing to function, and laid out a dozen cups and saucers on a tray. She heard the door open, and turned to see Michael coming in, and at the sight of his face she felt her heart give a leap of fear. He looked deathly pale, and his strong figure seemed to sag. His skin had a sallow look, and in his eyes was a look she could not meet.

He walked across the room and stood looking down unseeingly at the water heating on the stove.

"Did you"—Jody hesitated—"did you tell the police you'd seen Kennedy?"

He swung round to face her.

"Who told you I'd seen Kennedy?"

"Desmond and I saw you."

"So you went back again after leaving Kennedy?" he asked slowly.

"Yes. I wanted to know who was going to keep the appointment with him."

"Well, you found out," said Michael.

"After I'd seen you with him, I went to see Aunt Essie. She told me that Kennedy had sent for you to—"

"—to tell me that you were in danger. And I told him I hadn't the slightest influence with you and wouldn't be able to induce you to go away. And so he went to see her. And I," he ended slowly, "I went to see Laurie."

"You . . . went to see her!"

"I went to try and see her," he amended.

"How did you—"

"—know where she was? Kennedy told me where to look—
but he also told me that there wasn't much chance of her
being there. But I went."

"She . . . she threatened Fenella. . . ."

"That was only one of her threats. She'd made several.
The address Kennedy gave me was in Brook Street. I went
there. It seemed a decent place—open and aboveboard—nothing sinister. A woman came to the door and said that a Mrs.
Grierson had been staying there, but had left that day. I
asked where she'd gone."

"Kenya?"

"No. The address she'd given them when she left was
Dorset Court. I didn't believe I'd find her there, but I . . . I
decided to try. So I went there. I spent some time there, asking, looking and asking again. No sign. Then I went into a
sort of café and bought some sandwiches and ate them in
the car on the way home. It doesn't make a very convincing
story for the police."

He walked to the door and then looked back at her.

"I'm sorry about the beginning of all this," he said.

"The beginning—"

"You wanted to talk—but nobody would listen. I wish to
God . . ." He stopped and then spoke more quietly.
"Charles is on his way back. The police checked. He left
Saint-Malo about sixteen hours ago and he ought to make
Newhaven this morning."

"The police checked? But . . . but why?"

"Because Laurie was shot with his gun. They found it on
the grass between here and the cottages. Not hidden; just
lying there. So the police checked—and found that if Charles
had fired the shot, he would have had to do it from the middle of the Channel, because that's where he was."

"But . . . Charles doesn't keep the gun—"

"Here? I know that. The police know it too. Somebody
took it off *Gazelle*."

"But . . ."

"And the only person who goes regularly between here
and Marcove is the Major. I know that—and so do the police."

"Michael—"

She stopped. He had gone out and closed the door behind him.

Jody, left alone, went on performing mechanically tasks that were normal and everyday and entirely unconnected with mystery and death and horror. She forced herself to concentrate on what she was doing.

Hot coffee . . . milk . . . cream . . . brandy. A tray, and all was ready. Coffee was ready; come and get it. No, it was to be carried in. Into the hall, perhaps, where the three quiet policemen were seated, questioning, questioning . . .

Questioning Michael, who had tried to find Laurie, who had threatened his child. Asking Michael why he had come home so late. Asking how the gun, which was Charles's, had killed the woman called Laurie. Questioning . . . and noting the answers. Michael, Charles . . .

She made an effort to control the trembling that had seized her, but she knew that she had not the strength to lift the tray. And then the door opened and Estelle came in, and for a moment she thought that Estelle might carry the tray. But then she saw her face.

Estelle was standing in the doorway, swaying. Jody rushed to her and put round her arms that were now strong and steady. She led her to a chair and placed her in it and poured a cup of hot coffee and brought it to her.

"Drink that," she ordered. "You're faint, and no wonder. Go on—drink it." She drew up another chair and sat on it, talking with a calmness and reassurance that filled her with wonder.

"Drink it, Estelle darling. There's nothing to worry about. The woman who died . . . I'm sorry for her, but I think we're all going to be safer now that she's dead. I don't understand anything, but—"

"Michael," brought out Estelle in a choked voice.

"I know. He went to see her and the police—"

"They've taken him away."

Jody found herself on her feet.

"They've . . ."

Estelle was babbling almost incoherently.

"They've taken him away—the police. They've taken him away. In a car. With the Major. They've taken them both, and Miss Bishop—"

"Taken all three?"

"No. Taken Michael and the M-Major. Miss Bishop has . . I think she's fainted. The Professor's looking after her nd I came . . . I came . . ."

"Have they gone?"

"Y-yes. They went away—in a car. Two cars. One car with M-Michael and the other with the M-Major. And the police. The police . . ."

She had risen, and Jody forced her as gently as possible back into her chair.

"Drink that coffee—do you hear?" she said. She poured a liberal amount of brandy into the hot liquid. "Before you say nother word—drink that."

With shaking hands, Estelle lifted the cup. She sipped, nd sipped again, and Jody watched her.

"Go on—finish it," she said.

Estelle finished it, and put down the cup.

"Now," said Jody. "Can you tell me what happened?"

Estelle's lips trembled, but she made an effort to speak steadily.

"The police . . . the three of them . . . told me they wouldn't want me any more. Or Miss Bishop, or the Professor. But they . . . they would have to take away the Major and—and—"

"Go on."

"And Michael."

"For what?"

"For . . . for further questioning. And . . ."

"And what?"

"Michael left a message for you. He says that you're to go to Marcove and tell Charles—"

"But Charles is going to Newhaven."

"Go to Marcove, Michael says, and intercept him. Tell him what's happened. Tell him everything, Michael said. Jody"—her voice was agonized—"what'll they do to Michael? They can't believe that he had anything to do with . . . to do . . ."

"No," said Jody steadily. "All they want from Michael and the Major is what they said they wanted: more details."

"They've arrested them. Jody, they've arrested them! Jody . . ."

Once more, Jody succeeded in calming her. But her thoughts were not on what she was doing. They were with

Michael, who had become entangled in the net in which she herself had been the first to be caught. Michael—and the Major.

She remembered Miss Bishop, left with nobody to comfort her but the Professor. She led Estelle upstairs and made her lie down, saw that Fenella still slept and went down to the drawing room.

Miss Bishop was unconscious, lying in an untidy heap beside the fireplace. Beside her knelt the Professor, holding one of her hands and muttering soft, meaningless phrases in German. He relinquished his charge with open relief to Jody and hurried hither and thither obeying orders, bringing brandy, pushing up the sofa and helping to lift onto it the reviving Miss Bishop.

She lay quietly, her eyes on Jody. Memory returned slowly, and now and then a shudder went through her. When she spoke at last, it was in a voice almost dead with despair.

"They . . . they took him away," she said, and Jody knew that she did not mean Michael.

"Only for questioning." Jody put all the comfort she could into the words. "They'll let him—they'll let them come back soon, Miss Bishop. Please don't worry."

"It's no use." Miss Bishop's voice was calm. "They know. He tried to hide it from them, but they knew. They knew before he told them."

"Knew?" Jody tried to keep herself from trembling. "What did they know?"

"They knew that he . . . that my cousin had been in prison. They knew. When he came to the school, I didn't know. I had written to him and told him that I could get him a post on the staff, and I . . . he came, and there was no post for him. But he wouldn't go away. When I . . . when I insisted, he . . . he told me that he had just come out of prison. He had been in prison for—for two years. False pretenses, he said. He wanted to stay at the school and he said he wouldn't give any trouble. He said that if I insisted on his going away, he would tell everybody that he was . . . that he had . . ."

The Professor's gentle, admonishing voice broke into the tumbling sentences.

"You must not speak any more," he said. His long white hand reached out and patted Miss Bishop's shoulder. "Now at this time, you are not your right self, and you must not say things that you will be sorry for afterwards. Rest," he said gently. "Close your eyes and be patient and this thing will come the right way soon. You must only be patient and not say these things that you will remember afterwards."

Miss Bishop's eyes closed; she seemed to understand the wisdom of what the Professor had said. By signs, Jody indicated to him that there was coffee in the kitchen, and he hurried away, returning a little later with two cups. He drank one, and Jody by degrees persuaded Miss Bishop to sit up and drink the other. She had almost finished it when the Professor spoke again.

"Try to sleep," he urged. "I am going away to dress, but I will come back soon. Try to sleep."

Miss Bishop lay back obediently and her eyes closed. She seemed to be groping for something, and Jody clasped the restless hands firmly.

"Go to sleep," she said gently.

"Yes. Yes, I'll try." Miss Bishop's voice was thick, and Jody saw with relief that exhaustion had overcome her at last. "I'll try." Her eyes opened and attempted to focus on Jody. "D-don't go away."

"I won't. Go to sleep."

"Stay with me. P—promise."

"You shan't be alone, I promise."

Miss Bishop's eyes closed; her breathing became slow and heavy, but Jody sat on unmoving. When the Professor returned she would give up her place to him and go and look after Estelle.

Her mind felt dull; only one thing came back with more and more force and clarity: her need to see, to speak to Desmond. She wanted him. She longed for his presence, longed to hear his voice, longed to feel his hands on her own. In all her life she could not remember longing for anything with this singleness and intensity.

She glanced at her watch: six-thirty. It was not the time to wake Lady Wigram's household with a telephone call. Six-thirty . . . more than six hours since she had opened the door and stepped outside to speak to Laurie. And Laurie was dead, her slender body shrouded and carried away to lie in a mortuary. . . .

She looked up to find Estelle coming into the room. She was fully dressed, and to Jody's relief, quiet and calm.

"As soon as you feel it's reasonable time," she told Jody, "I'm going to drive to Nancy Wigram's. I want to leave Fenella with her for today."

"Wouldn't you prefer to keep Fenella with you?"

"No. She'll be better with Nancy's children—and I shall be free to go and see Michael. And you'll be able to go and find Charles." Her voice faltered for a moment. "I wish he hadn't gone away."

She looked up as the Professor came in, and managed to smile at him.

"You are not going to sleep a little?" he asked her anxiously. "You should, I think."

"I can't sleep. I'm going to take Fenella over to the Wigrams as soon as I can."

"That is a good idea," said the Professor. "Why do you not stay there yourself?"

"No. I want to be near my husband, if they . . . if they'll let me. But I'll have to take the car," she told him, "and Jody has to go to Marcove. If you could let her use your car—"

"No," said Jody. "I'll take Miss Bishop's."

"If I may offer myself, I shall be happy to drive you," the Professor told her.

Jody, remembering his appalling driving and longing to refuse, changed her mind and said nothing. For a short while at any rate, she reflected, fears for her own safety would drive out all other thoughts.

Miss Bishop woke at about half-past seven, and sat up to weary and disheveled realization of what the day was to bring to all of them. To Estelle's suggestion of driving with her to the Wigram's and then going on to see the Major, she gave an eager, pathetically grateful assent. She went to the cottage to tidy herself and once more Jody found herself making coffee.

"You should have slept a little," Estelle told her in a worried voice. "You look so pale."

"We'll sleep when this is over," said Jody.

She went out into the hall, and to the telephone. It was not, now, too early to speak to Desmond. She longed to pour out the history of the terrible night, and to hear his assurance that soon he would be with her.

She heard Lady Wigram's voice, and apologized for the early call. She said nothing of the night's happenings, stating simply that Estelle was anxious to bring Fenella over and leave her for the day. Lady Wigram's voice was warm with pleasure; no time was too early, she said; the boys were already up and about and would look forward to seeing Fenella.

And finally, asked Jody, was Desmond up? She would like a word with him.

"Desmond?" His sister sounded surprised. "Desmond isn't here."

"Not . . . not there?"

"No. He didn't come back last night."

"Didn't . . . come back?"

"No. He rang up and said he'd decided to spend the night at his club."

"Rang up? What time?"

"I can't quite remember. It was late," recalled Lady Wigram. "It was just before midnight, I think. He rang up from a call box and said I wasn't to expect him home until I actually saw him."

"He didn't say . . ."

"He didn't say any more than that. I was just going to ask you if you knew where he'd gone off to."

"No. No, I don't," said Jody.

She put down the receiver and stood still. He had not gone home. He had left her, and he had gone straight to a call box and had told his sister that he would not be home that night. He had gone—where?—without a word. He had kissed her—and he had gone away.

She heard the Professor's voice, and saw him at the front door, an overcoat on his arm, a battered hat in his hand, a tattered wollen muffler dangling from one of his pockets.

"I am ready," he told her. "My car is here. But there is no hurry for you."

She went upstairs and washed and tidied herself. Then she went downstairs, and the Professor led her to his car, struggled with the door and ushered Jody into the antiquated interior. He took his place at the wheel, and peered uncertainly at the gear lever.

"Would you like me to drive?" asked Jody, without hope.

"No." The Professor gave a soft laugh. "No, no, no. This car is only for me—it is not for others. It is like a naughty person in a hospital, who will do something only for one nurse."

The nurse was almost terrifyingly incompetent. Jody, not as a rule a nervous driver, found herself alternatively clenching her fists tightly in her lap, and clinging to the stuffing that protruded from the cushions. This proving an inadequate support, she braced her feet against imaginary brakes, and pressed them as oncoming traffic bore down upon them and missed them by inches. The Professor's hat was drawn down on his head; his muffler was wound round his neck and his coat was spread over Jody's knees. He stared straight ahead, lips compressed, his knuckles white with the tenseness of his grip on the steering wheel.

He did not speak until they were nearing the Cove. Then: "You think," he asked, "that already Charles will be here?"

"I don't know. If he isn't, he'll be near. When I see him, I'll take *Gazelle* out and meet him."

"*Gazelle?* He is not—"

"He took *Ballerina;* he was going to buy her from the. . ."

She could not bring herself to say the Major's name. The Major was no longer offering boats for sale. He was in the hands of the police, he and Michael. . . .

"But why should you go to meet him?"

"I'm going to stop him from going to Newhaven."

"*Gazelle* is not too big for you to take?"

"No. I can manage."

"You cannot go alone." The Professor's voice quavered, but he repeated the words in a firmer voice. "You cannot go alone. If you wish to go out to Charles, I shall come with you."

Jody knew what the offer must have cost him. His fear of boats, of the sea, was well-known. She saw that even the possibility of venturing on the water had made him as pale as death.

"It's very kind of you," she said firmly, "but I'll manage by myself. I know how you hate the sea. I'll be all right."

"No. Other days, yes. But today you have received a shock," said the Professor. "Today is different."

Today was different, acknowledged Jody to herself.

But when they reached Marcove and stood at the cliff top looking down at the little harbor, the day did not look different from other days. All trace of the recent storm had gone; the water was as calm as it had been on countless other summer mornings when she had come down here with

Charles, to sail with him or to see him off. There had been other skies as clear and as blue, other mornings when the surface of the sea was almost mirror-still. Now, as they stood, they could see the wide expanse of Channel and the white sails of yachts that seemed scarcely to move. Shading her eyes, Jody let them move along the surface of the sea, looking for *Ballerina*'s familiar lines.

It was long, however, before she came into view. An hour passed, two, three. They sat now in the car, now on a bench outside the Tar Barrel, drinking coffee, saying nothing, waiting. . . .

And then at last, Jody stood up.

"There she is."

She began to walk down the steep slope, and the Professor stumbled along by her side. When they reached *Gazelle*, she glanced at him and saw that he was white with fear.

"You mustn't come with me," she said firmly. "I shall be quite all right by myself."

She had no desire for his company, and for a moment, watching him, she hoped that fear might conquer kindness—and then she saw that his silence was due to the fact that he was nerving himself to step on board.

"Won't you stay here?" she asked for the last time.

He shook his head.

"No. I am very afraid," he confessed, "but I shall come. Please do not notice me; I shall not give you trouble. But if I let you go alone, I shall not feel that I am doing what is right."

"We should reach *Ballerina* in half an hour—Charles will see us and come to meet us. The sea's dead calm."

Dead . . . and calm. Dead, like the woman who had fallen at her feet on the steps. Calm, like Laurie, lying in a mortuary. The sea's calm would be succeeded by movement—but Laurie would still be dead . . . dead, forever unmoving.

Her mind went to Desmond, and once more the longing for him swept over her. With an effort, she brought her mind to the Professor, and helped him aboard and prepared to take *Gazelle* to sea.

She would see Charles—and she would have to tell him not only the terrible news of the night that was just gone, but the whole of the events leading up to it. She would tell him about Desmond, and of her feelings for Desmond.

She looked ahead. *Ballerina* was drawing closer, and she

knew that Charles must have seen her. He was coming—and for the first time, she seemed to see their relationship with all its inadequacies, all its imperfections. There had been liking, but no love; pleasure in one another's society, but no passion. They had drawn together, as they were drawing together now; meeting, but not merging.

*Ballerina* came on, light and graceful like the dancer that she was. She glanced at the Professor, and was relieved to find that he was no longer crouching fearfully against the rail. He was standing and watching, as she was watching, the approach of *Ballerina*. The boats neared one another: she could see Charles busy with ropes, and she waited for his attention to become disengaged so that she could call to him. Far away were isolated fishing boats. Beyond them, a large liner moved lazily; nearer at hand, a small naval patrol vessel sped swiftly, leaving a lacy white train trailing in the water.

Jody took a firm grip on the helm, waiting for Charles's order.

And then she felt the grip of two hands closing over her throat.

The sea vanished, and became the sky. Her hands, torn from the wheel, waved wildly, helplessly, and then fastened on the hands that gripped her, and she tore and clawed at them and knew that she could not move them. Their grip was tightening . . . tightening. . . .

Thought ceased, and instinct took its place. Her feet, lifted off the deck, flailed and found something against which to press. The hands were jerked away, and she was falling—and then for one moment she lay and saw the Professor's face swooping down, his hands, like talons, tensed to grip once more.

The Professor, and his long, white hands. The Professor, with blue eyes no longer mild, but hard with the hardness and glaze of china. The Professor's fingers round her throat, pressing, pressing. . . .

Once more she had torn herself free, only to be brought down with brutal force onto the deck. She fought, and knew that the struggle would be brief; Charles was near, but not near enough. Air . . . there was no air. There was no sky. There was only black terror and despair and the knowledge that soon she would be able to fight no longer.

She felt darkness closing in upon her, and made a last desperate effort to free herself—and then she saw that the darkness was moving and breaking up and parting as a shape, large and growing larger, appearing between *Gazelle* and the sun, hanging for an instant over the little ship and then sweeping by. *Gazelle*, left rocking wildly in a boiling sea, plunged, dipped, and then heeled over, and a cry from Jody ended in a gasp as she was hurled into the sea.

As she hit the water and went under, she knew that she was safe from the Professor. Kicking her way to the surface, she told herself that Charles had chosen the swiftest, the surest way to save her: he had driven *Ballerina* into *Gazelle*.

And then, surfacing, she shook the water from her eyes and realized that *Ballerina* was nowhere to be seen. Close to her, *Gazelle* lay on her side, her sails trailing in the sea. Some distance beyond, the Professor was struggling desperately in the water. And turning in a half-circle of bubbling white froth was the naval patrol vessel—and as it bore down upon them Jody over its wake saw *Ballerina*, and upon *Ballerina*'s deck, Charles.

Charles . . .

Charles, watching. Charles, listening to her cries and disregarding them. Charles, motionless upon the deck of *Ballerina*, watching dispassionately the Professor fighting for life a rope's length away.

Charles . . .

He turned his gaze on her as she began to swim toward the Professor—and then he had glanced away to watch the man who had dived from the naval vessel and was swimming strongly toward Jody.

The man reached her, put out a strong arm and gathered her to him and held her, but she twisted herself out of his hold.

"Desmond—the Professor! He can't swim! He—"

"It's all right, Jody. Charles is near and—"

"No!" The sound was a wail of despair. "No, he . . . he isn't going to . . ."

She saw Desmond turn in the water and look back. The Professor was no longer struggling.

"Go to him—I'm all right. Oh, go to him!" Jody begged.

She saw Desmond swimming away from her, swimming strongly and swiftly, but she knew that he would not reach the Professor in time. And Charles, who had been near, who could have saved him . . . Charles had watched and had done nothing.

She half-swam, half-drifted to *Gazelle* and hung there, her eyes closed. When she opened them, there was no sign of the Professor. She saw Desmond, after a time, turn and come back to her. She saw the patrol vessel coming nearer; she saw *Ballerina* moving away, not in the direction of Newhaven, not in the direction of Marcove, but out to sea. *Ballerina*, with Charles aboard, was going . . .

She was in Desmond's arms. So much she knew, but no more. She heard a confusion of sounds, but she did not open her eyes. She heard voices. Gentle hands raised her, held her.

Opening her eyes at last, she saw blue sky framing the white, wet, stricken face of Desmond Huntley. Behind him on the deck of the patrol vessel was another man, and Jody turned a leaden gaze toward him.

It was Mr. Kennedy.

# CHAPTER
# 16

It was very quiet in the room. It was a strange room, and Jody was glad, for familiar things brought to her mind memories which she could not yet face.

It was a tidy room; not large. A man's room; a wide desk, hide-covered chairs, dark, heavy curtains and a faint haze of smoke. There were only two people in the room: Jody, and the man, facing one another across the desk.

"If you would rather hear some of it at some other time—" began Mr. Kennedy.

"No."

"I brought you here because I felt that we could talk better alone. The others know all there is to know, but you were not well enough to—"

"Please go on."

Mr. Kennedy rose, poured out a drink and carried it to her.

"Take some of this," he said. "And then lean back and listen quietly and I'll make it as brief as I can."

"Go on, please."

"I shall never forgive myself," he said, "for not having told you who I was. But it seemed to me then that what I did was right. Looking back . . . I don't know. . . . But you shall soon hear why I could not be frank with you."

Jody waited.

"I was acting in the dark," went on Mr. Kennedy. "You and Huntley came to Dorset Court and the clerk made his report to me. I was there from the C.I.D. purely by chance, to see if the man we'd placed there had learned anything. He hadn't. The Griersons had left no trace, and nothing more had been learned about them. When the clerk came to me, I followed you both out to the car. I saw two young people who looked all right, but who had come inquiring about a woman with a shady record in more than one country. You

173

might have been straight—but who can judge by appearances? I had to be sure."

"And so you searched my aunt's house for—"

"Yes. That told us little—but later, I located Laurie. I could have held her, but I didn't; she was of far more use to us while she was free. But I had to make sure that you and the Commander had no connection with her—and so I got you both to the Merlin, and arranged to meet Laurie there. Two police officers were close to you; they watched you when she came in, and they heard what you said. It was clear that neither of you knew her. Having made certain of that, I . . . I began to worry about you. I was sorry that I had aroused your curiosity. I was sorry that . . . but perhaps, in the end, nothing that I said or did made any difference."

He paused, and pushed toward her the drink she had put down on the desk. When she had drunk a little, he resumed his story.

"I shall tell you exactly what happened when you went that morning to Dorset Court. The Professor was there. On his visits to his Conservatoire at Harrogate, he always called at Dorset Court—Number Four. He went there on his way up, and he went there on his way back to the school. He saw you come in. You had your equipment and he knew that you were going to give somebody in the building one of your beauty treatments; you were on your way to a client, and all he had to do was to keep out of your way. But presently, he began to worry. He saw in what direction you were going, and he realized that by some extraordinary error, you were going to Number Four. He had at all costs to stop you. He did. He crept up behind you as you looked through the window in the corridor, and he hit you. Then he carried you into the apartment and—"

"And laid me on the carpet."

"Yes. You were only there for a few moments, while he discussed what should be done with you. Then you were carried to the foot of the stairs and left there. The door of the elevator was left open, ensuring that nobody could use it. A telephone call was put through from another floor, reporting the elevator out of order. An engineer was sent at once, and he found you. The manager reported the matter to the police in a purely routine way—but when I saw the report, I went to Dorset Court. But by that time, the Griersons had vanished, and so had our link with an international gang of smugglers."

"Smugglers?"

"Yes. They operated," said Mr. Kennedy, "on the grand scale. Watches. Hundreds, thousands of watches pouring in from the Continent and finding their way into this country—undetected. We didn't know how they came in. All we knew at first was that they were distributed from the Joachim Conservatoire at Harrogate."

"Laurie—"

"She had been working in France, living with one of the members of the organization. He was caught by the French police, and convicted, and Laurie crossed the Channel. And so, for the first time, we had a tie-up between the Continental gang, and the gang here in England. Laurie went straight up to Harrogate, and that was when the Joachim Conservatoire first came to our notice. But for some time, we couldn't get any further."

"Then one day," went on Mr. Kennedy, "there was an accident. Not the accident that happened to you. There was a car smash in Sussex, and two men were killed—two men who had been working for the Professor. Their deaths left him without two key men—and he decided to come south and take the place of one of them, the man who had been the music master at the boys' school called Broome Abbey.

"He brought Laurie as far as London, and put her into a flat in Dorset Court, with strict orders that she was never on any pretext whatsoever to venture into Sussex. She agreed, and she stuck to the agreement . . . until you came into the picture. You came by accident, and you brought disaster."

"I don't—"

"You don't yet see why. I shall tell you. Number Four Dorset Court had become a link in the chain that stretched from Harrogate to Broome, and your accident forced the Professor to give up the apartment. It had been impossible, without risk of being seen by someone, to move you right away from Number Four while you were unconscious, and he was afraid that an investigation might take place and bring him too close to the police. He decided that the apartment should be given up—in a hurry. It was vacated, and the direct result was that Laurie was left homeless. And . . . she decided to go south. That was a mistake, and she paid for it with her life.

"I didn't know she had called at the school. She went in fear of the Professor; so much I knew from my talks with her. But something stronger than fear took her to Broome. I didn't know she had been there, and I didn't learn the fact until I spoke to you at the Merlin after you had seen me at the rendezvous that I had made with your brother-in-law."

"Why did you—?"

"Why did I want to see him? I sent for your brother-in-law because Miss Bishop had gone to the police with some important information."

"Miss Bishop!"

"She played a game of hide-and-seek with your little niece, Fenella, and hid from her—in the study. The Professor had been in the room, playing his cello, and then he was persuaded—against his will, if you remember—to go into the drawing room for a drink. He would have liked to put his cello away—but that would have looked odd, and so he had to leave it, and its case. But he could be almost sure that nobody would go into the room in the short time that he was away from it.

"But—Fenella went in. She hid herself from Miss Bishop. And Miss Bishop found her . . . in the Professor's empty cello case. Little girls playing a game are not very careful how they handle things; the case had been subjected to some rather rough treatment, and when Miss Bishop found Fenella, she also found the resting-place of several hundred watches."

"And that is why she—"

"—was taken ill? Yes. When she recovered, she went first to her cousin, Major Miller. She was certain that he had something to do with what was going on. The Major denied all knowledge of the matter, and Miss Bishop felt that she was left with two alternatives: to tell the Headmaster, or to tell the police. She decided to tell us. When I heard her story, I telephoned for your brother-in-law, and he came up to meet me—but before I could see him, I saw you, and learned from you that Laurie had visited the school. And when I heard that, I knew that you were the reason for her going there, and I knew that she would stop at nothing to get you out of the way."

"But . . . but why? Why?"

"Please be patient; you will learn in a moment. Miss Bishop's discovery told the police nothing that they had not known before. We already knew that the Professor was the head of the organization, receiving the watches and carrying them up to Harrogate. What we didn't know for certain was . . . who was bringing them to Broome? The night before Miss Bishop saw the cello case, I had been down to have a talk with Major Miller. He said that he knew nothing—but my visit frightened him. Miss Bishop's discovery frightened him still more, and so the next time he went to Marcove, he brought back with him the gun that Charles Vaughan had left on *Gazelle*. If he had hidden it securely when he got home . . . but he didn't. He put it in his hall, where it could be seen by anybody who passed the house."

"But he . . ."

"No, he didn't shoot Laurie. When Laurie knocked on your door, the Major was asleep in his chair. But the Professor was awake. He was upstairs, and he must, I think, have seen Laurie waiting for you. He went out of the cottage and saw, through the uncurtained window of the Major's sitting room, that the Major was asleep. He went in—and took the gun, and what woke the Major was the sound of the shot. It woke him—and he was in time to see the Professor running back to his cottage before emerging again, as if newly roused from sleep, feeling his way over to see what had happened."

There was a long silence.

"With Laurie's death," resumed Mr. Kennedy after a time, "we knew that the Professor was finished. And the Professor knew it too. But what we had to do was to force his hand; we wanted him to lead us to the man who had brought the supplies into the country. We had to have more than theories—we had to have proof.

"We arrested your brother-in-law and the Major. We took your brother-in-law in order to leave the Professor a clear field; we took the Major because we were still not sure of him. But we knew that when we had made the arrests, the Professor would have to act. And when he acted, we would know who his accomplice was."

Jody's eyes were fixed unseeingly on the neat papers on the desk. Mr. Kennedy's voice did not change.

"I told you," he said quietly, "that two people died in that car smash. The music master—and one other. That other was a man vital to the organization, because he was the man responsible for getting the goods into England. He had to be a splendid seaman. He had to own a boat and he had to sail out in all seasons and in all weathers to meet, off Newhaven, the cross-Channel steamer—the Newhaven-Dieppe steamer. On the steamer, a man would come up on deck, identify the little boat, and with apparent carelessness throw overboard a bundle of what looked like rubbish. Some of the rubbish would sink—but some of it wouldn't. And if anyone happened to be sailing by, why should they be suspicious if they saw a man in a small boat picking up something from the sea? You can understand, can you not, the importance of this man to the Professor? Without him, the organization could not operate."

Tears—the first she had shed since the terrible events that had taken place forty-eight hours ago—welled up in Jody's eyes and rolled slowly down her cheeks. Looking up, she met Mr. Kennedy's eyes and saw in them sadness and a great compassion. She put out a hand gropingly and he took it and held it fast.

"I think that at first," he said slowly, "the Professor must have considered approaching the Major. But the Major was a weak man—and the organization had no use for weak men. And so the Professor . . . went to Charles Vaughan."

The little clock on the desk ticked in the silence. Jody did not move.

"He invited Charles to the flat in Dorset Court," went on Mr. Kennedy. "And Charles and Laurie met. She fell in love with him, and he . . . I think that he loved you, but men are only men, and as you saw, she was beautiful."

"He . . ."

"He went by the name of Grierson, and they shared the apartment. He was there whenever his extra lessons took him to London. All this we knew, for the flat was watched—but we did not know enough to enable us to act.

"And then, by an extraordinary and—for Charles Vaughan —tragic turn of Fate, you went to the apartment on a day that he was there. The Professor saw you. The Professor knew that if you went to Number Four and rang the bell, the door would be opened by your fiancé, Charles Vaughan, in a dressing gown.

"So the Professor acted—and in the confusion that followed, Laurie learned something that nobody had thought it necessary, or wise, to tell her before: that Charles was engaged to you. She was sick of London, sick of the organi-

ration, sick of the Professor. She only wanted one thing:
Charles Vaughan. And so she ignored the Professor's warning,
and she went to Sussex. And that led us a little closer to
Charles Vaughan, but we could still not be sure of how far he
was involved. She was a beautiful woman, and his interest
might have been solely in her. We knew the Major's history:
he Major was the more likely link. We had to have proof.

"Laurie went down to Broome to look for you. You were
in the way, and she wanted you out of the way. She found
you, and she saw no reason why you should not learn some
of the truth—and that is why she died.

"Afterwards, the Professor went out with you to meet
Charles Vaughan, and then—like Laurie—he made a mistake:
he misjudged Vaughan. He thought that by killing you, he
would leave Charles with only one course open to him: to
cross the Channel and continue operations on the other side.
So he decided to kill you."

There was a pause. Mr. Kennedy left Jody's side and
walked slowly up and down the room, and then halted once
more beside her chair.

"Perhaps you understand now," he said, "why I could not
tell you that the police were interested in your accident at
Dorset Court. If Vaughan or the Professor . . ."

"Yes, I understand," said Jody.

"But at the end," said Mr. Kennedy, "it was I who made a
mistake. A serious mistake. I didn't think of the sea approach. It was Huntley who thought of that. When you took
him to Lady Cleeve's flat and she told you about my visit, he
knew that she was keeping something back. She told you
that I had brought the papers as an excuse, in case you were
with her. Huntley realized that that meant that I had said
something to her which I did not want passed on to you. So
when he left you, he drove straight back to London and
roused your aunt from her bed and asked for the truth—and
she told him all that I had told her. And what I had told her
was that it was almost certain that the Professor's accomplice
was not the Major . . . but Charles Vaughan.

"Huntley left her and went down to Portsmouth and got
hold of a naval friend of his who commanded a fast patrol
boat. They went on an unofficial trip. Before he went, he
told Lady Cleeve to get in touch with me and tell me what
he was doing. When I knew, I went out on a police launch
and got aboard the patrol boat. Huntley didn't want me. His

idea was to contact Charles Vaughan and give him a chance to get out—if he wanted to. But . . . that wasn't quite how things worked out. I leave you to imagine what I felt when we neared *Gazelle* and saw . . ."

Once more he stopped. Silence fell, and it was a long time before Jody broke it.

"*Ballerina—*" she began at last, and paused.

"—has not been traced," said Mr. Kennedy. "I think that Charles Vaughan sailed her to France, and I do not think that he will ever return." His voice deepened. "A man without a country. . . . But perhaps it was as well, Jody. There was not much for Vaughan to come home to."

He waited for questions, but there were none. After a moment, he went slowly out of the room and closed the door behind him.

## CHAPTER

# 17

ITALY WAS HOT, Spain an inferno. Lady Cleeve, who liked
always to be cool, bore the discomfort for her niece's sake,
but she was greatly and opening relieved when Jody, at the
end of August, proposed returning home.

"But we haven't been to Granada," pointed out her aunt
conscientiously. "Or Cordoba."

"I know. Let's go home," said Jody.

"We've paid for a trip to Tangier."

"We can get the money back. Let's go home."

"And didn't you want to meet those people at Jerez de la
Frontera?"

"Not any more. Let's go home."

They went home, and arrived on the day before Jody's
birthday.

"Stay with me and have it here," begged her aunt.

So Jody stayed at the house in Knightsbridge. When she
awoke next morning, the table in her room was gay with
brightly colored parcels. Gifts from Estelle and Michael and
the children, a posy from the Major, a hand-knitted scarf
from Miss Bishop.

But there was nothing from Desmond Huntley.

There was no letter, no telegram, no gift—and no telephone call.

His leave, she knew, was over. Though she had heard
nothing from him herself, her aunt had told her that he was
in England again after a short spell of duty in the Mediterra-
nean. He might, Jody told herself, have been sent away
again. If he was sent, he would have to go. He could not be
where he wanted to be . . . where she wanted him to be.

But throughout her trip, there had been no letters, no
messages . . . nothing.

She went up to her room before lunch, having waited in
vain for a sign. Standing in the middle of the room, she

pressed her hands together and told herself that the Navy was a busy life, and . . .

No message. Not even a little goat.

Her throat felt dry. She wanted him, longed for him with a desperate longing. She needed him.

With an effort, she fought down uneasiness and began to fold the papers that had been wrapped round her birthday presents.

Twenty-five. She was twenty-five, and she had had a great many presents; every present but one.

She heard her aunt's footsteps and went to the door. Lady Cleeve stood on the threshold, on her face a look difficult for Jody to analyze.

"Somebody wants to see you," she told Jody.

Jody's heart leapt.

"Downstairs?"

"Outside."

"*Outside?* Won't he . . . won't they come in?"

"It's not a they, it's a he. And he can't come in. He says you're to look out of the window."

"Out of the . . ."

"Yes. This window."

The window opened on to the street. Jody walked to it and looked out.

Down in the heart of Knightsbridge, a small and attentive crowd watched a very large man trying to lead a very small, white and reluctant goat up to the little house. The goat wore a huge pink bow round its neck, and round its middle was a pink sash on which was emblazoned the words: BETSY II.

He looked up, and saw Jody, and she wished that she had wings to fly out, fly down and tell him of her gratitude. He would not let her harbor unhappy pictures. He would not let her nurse dark memories. Here, in proof, was his reminder that the past was the past, and what had happened had brought them together.

He was calling up to her.

"Happy Birthday." He wagged a finger at Betsy. "For you. Shall I bring her up?"

Jody waited until she could speak steadily.

"No. I'm coming down," she said.

# EMILIE LORING

Women of all ages are falling under the enchanting spell Emilie Loring weaves in her beautiful novels. She fills each book with powerful drama and makes every story an unforgettable experience. Enter the romantic world of Emilie Loring. Once you have finished one book by her, you will surely want to read them all.

| | |
|---|---|
| SPRING ALWAYS COMES | HL4543 |
| HOW CAN THE HEART FORGET | HL4510 |
| BECKONING TRAILS | HL4515 |
| THE TRAIL OF CONFLICT | HL4283 |
| A CERTAIN CROSSROAD | HL4251 |
| THE SOLITARY HORSEMAN | HL4224 |
| TO LOVE AND TO HONOR | HL4511 |
| A CANDLE IN HER HEART | HL4526 |
| UNCHARTED SEAS | HL4531 |
| HILLTOPS CLEAR | HL4536 |
| GAY COURAGE | HL4190 |
| SWIFT WATER | HL4211 |
| FOREVER AND A DAY | HL4534 |
| WITH BANNERS | HL4532 |
| IT'S A GREAT WORLD | HL4528 |
| BRIGHT SKIES | HL4516 |
| LIGHTED WINDOWS | HL4535 |
| FAIR TOMORROW | HL4537 |
| WE RIDE THE GALE | HL4527 |
| AS LONG AS I LIVE | HL4533 |
| HIGH OF HEART | HL4530 |
| THROW WIDE THE DOOR | HL4514 |
| THERE IS ALWAYS LOVE | HL4517 |
| KEEPERS OF THE FAITH | HL4519 |
| RAINBOW AT DUSK | HL4522 |
| WHEN HEARTS ARE LIGHT AGAIN | HL4523 |
| GIVE ME ONE SUMMER | HL4529 |

*Now just 60¢ each!*

**Ask for them at your local bookseller or use this handy coupon:**

Bantam Books, Inc., Dept. EL, Room 300, 271 Madison Ave., N. Y., N. Y. 10016.

Please send me the titles I have checked.

Name_____

Address_____

City_____State_____Zip Code_____
(Please send check or money order. No currency or C.O.D.'s. Add 10¢ per book on orders of less than 5 books to cover the cost of postage and handling.) Please allow about four weeks for delivery.
EL-3/69

# If you think this book was good, wait 'til you see what *else* we've got in store for you!

## Send for your FREE catalog of Bantam Bestsellers today!

This money-saving catalog lists hundreds of best-sellers originally priced from $3.75 to $15.00—yours now in Bantam paperback editions for just 50¢ to $1.75! Here is a great opportunity to read the good books you've missed and add to your private library at huge savings! The catalog is FREE! So don't delay—send for yours today!

Ready for Mailing Now
Send for your FREE copy today

**BANTAM BOOKS, INC.**
Dept. GA3, 414 East Golf Road, Des Plaines, Ill.

I'm tired of paying high prices for good books. Please send me your latest free catalog of Bantam Books.

Name_____

Address_____

City_____State_____Zip_____

Please allow about four weeks for delivery

GA3—2/69